Barbara and Norman

Two Older Individuals, a Drag Queen and a Volvo

Andrew William James

CONTENTS

1. The Pickup

It was Friday, pension and weekly shop day. Barbara's heart sank when she awoke and realised her pension was now paid directly into her bank account. No longer did she have the pleasure of queueing at the Post Office and entering into chit-chat with the other pensioners, most of whom spent their time complaining about the price of TV stamps.

Secretly Barbara had quite enjoyed the feeling of being only-ever-so-slightly superior to her contemporaries. She had lived in London most of her life and therefore considered herself a cut above everyone else, even if that did mean having to queue for her pension. Barbara dressed conservatively and wore her shoulder-length greying hair loose. She was still an attractive woman with mischievous hazel eyes and a slender figure.

Looking out of her window, she thought to herself that today would have to be an umbrella day. It was supposed to be May but there was no sign of any improvement in the weather. She supposed this was due to being located on the east coast next to the North Sea.

Moving to Welling-by-the-Sea had seemed like a good idea at the time. She'd sold her flat and moved to be close to her family and achieve her lifelong dream of living next to the sea. Successive governments, package holidays and the general running down of the country meant that what should have been an ideal retirement had turned ever so slowly into a living nightmare.

The rest of Suffolk was doing very well apart from her little corner. How she hated that horrid little Beeching man who had deprived her and many others of the possibility of easily travelling around the country on a train. There had been talk of some of the lines in her own county reopening and she had rather foolishly based the decision to move on these rumours. Unfortunately, this didn't happen, and it was instead easier to drive to nearby towns rather than catch infrequent buses.

Two cups of tea and a chocolate digestive later saw Barbara behind the wheel of her car - and what a car, for it was one of the very last Volvo 340s which she had bought new upon retirement. She'd also had a towbar installed just in case she took up caravanning or needed to tow something. She'd chosen this particular model of car as it had a very noisy automatic gearbox and people generally got out of the way as it sounded like a bus descending on them. In other words, they heard the car before they saw it. She particularly enjoyed the look of panic on the faces of dog walkers.

She turned the key in the ignition and waited, turned again and Ruby fired into life. She selected reverse and eased out into the road.

Three minutes later and Barbara arrived at her destination. A shopping centre built to provide services to her local community sixty years ago, now struggling, like many other centres, against competition from the more modern, larger, out-of-town shopping destinations.

Barbara parked Ruby away from other cars. She couldn't afford any more dents and Ruby's ageing gearbox had a habit of lurching forward or backwards whenever moved between drive and reverse. Even neutral was a problem as the engine started revving up.

Parking further away meant a longer walk but she loved seeing the shopping spoils other people loaded into their cars. Barbara wondered how these people would survive without pizza and ready meals. She cleared her throat in a self-satisfied manner, safe in the knowledge that she, of course, cooked everything from scratch and ensured her meals were delicious, healthy, and balanced.

"How one feels for the younger generation," she thought. "Oh well, a problem for someone else to worry about."

As she approached the supermarket Barbara glanced at the outdoor dining area. Tables and chairs were arranged to allow the customers of several establishments to sit, eat or enjoy a coffee or something stronger. Barbara's eye was caught by someone new. She was both attracted and intrigued, he looked, dare she say, ever so slightly Hitchcock.

Her glance did not go unnoticed,

'May I be of assistance?' the man shouted out to her in a very boomy authoritarian voice.

'I don't know what you mean' she replied, 'I was just about to put my face mask on' and with that, she hurried into the supermarket to begin the arduous task of finding items in date until the next week.

Safely inside the supermarket, Barbara wondered who this newcomer was.

She didn't ponder for long as she noticed her timing was spot on and the yellow labels had just been placed on the fresh vegetables. Well, not so fresh as they were yesterday's but still plenty of bargains and this type of shopping allowed her to try out different foods and recipes. She noticed a new type of Broccoli that she had seen roasted on the television.

"I shall give that a try tonight," she thought, hoping the bits wouldn't get stuck in her teeth. It wasn't that she necessarily needed to save money, but, that she had been brought up in an age of frugality and she relished a bargain.

An hour later and Barbara had filled her trolley, she was now ready to depart the supermarket. She considered buying a lottery ticket for tomorrow night's draw but decided against it as she didn't want to start a gambling habit.

"Ahh", she thought, "how nice it would be to have a big win and go on a luxury cruise."

Her strategy of dropping hints to her nieces and nephews about the P&O Nordic cruises didn't seem to be working. Instead, they seemed to want help with putting down deposits on houses or buying cars or indeed their own luxury holidays. It completely mystified her as to why they wouldn't want to take her on a 10-day luxury cruise. Too busy, was the conclusion she came to.

Leaving the supermarket, Barbara noticed that the newcomer had left. This was rather opportune as it meant she could now get to her car without any more ridiculous heckling. She packed everything into the boot and returned her trolley.

Getting back into Ruby she started the engine and engaged reverse. For a short moment, she could have sworn she saw someone in a wheelchair in the rear-view mirror, but they were gone and she must have been mistaken. It was just as well since she was in a hurry and had a blemish-free advanced driver's licence for the past 50 years.

Ruby lurched backwards before being forced into drive whereupon she gave a massive jolt forward. Phew, she was now going in the right direction at least and managed to get enough speed up to shoot through the exit and onto the road without stopping.

Stopping and starting were particularly problematic, due to the slipping gearbox clutch. One cither accelerated hard and sometimes Ruby would respond or she would only respond once the revs were high resulting in the car lurching forward. Barbara had to chuckle as she drove past the bus stop, not only was it raining on the poor souls forced into taking public transport, but they seemed to be very angry, shouting at her car and pointing. She supposed they wanted a lift, but it would be impractical and, besides, you can't give just anyone a lift.

As she proceeded further up the road, she noticed that the schoolchildren were being particularly rude, laughing and pointing at her car. She blamed people's lack of manners on the demise of grammar schools. Never in her day would this sort of behaviour be tolerated. She assumed that poor old Ruby must be sounding particularly noisy today.

Barbara had discovered that playing Radio 3 at three-quarters level drowned out the whine of Ruby's gearbox. And so it was that with a flourish of Bizet's March of the Toreadors, Ruby came to a stop in her driveway. Now the problem was getting the ignition key, which often got stuck, to turn, so that she could switch the engine off. Bizet roared on and the key was still stuck. Barbara noticed two of her neighbours rushing to greet her. Annette Digby had retired from her job as a dinner lady in the local school. She still wore her now greying hair in a bun and instead of her white school apron she insisted on wearing a flowery house apron during the day. It was quite normal to see her with her cordless phone in her hand or, if she was really busy, in her apron. Annette loved nothing better than a good gossip with her neighbours. She'd heard some particularly juicy news about one of the church volunteers and the communion wine.

Her neighbour Lionel, a recently retired Vicar, was going grey and bald on top. Of medium height he had been piling on the pounds since he retired. The lack of mental stimulation meant that he had started to become forgetful. Since becoming forgetful he'd decided to wear his clerical collar during the day, it was comforting and afforded him certain privileges at the local Women's Institute run café. It also made him feel comfortable whenever he lent the new inexperienced vicar a hand in the running of the church, for which he received very little thanks. Lionel had also heard the news about the communion wine and wanted to assure Barbara that nothing was amiss. Barbara was, after all, a generous benefactor of the Church.

"How nice of my neighbours to greet me," she thought, "but totally unnecessary" She was more than capable of unloading her shopping and if she did need help there was always the offer from her fellow churchgoers.

Finally, the key in the barrel turned to the off position and the radio was silenced. As she opened the door, she hoped that she wouldn't have to engage in conversation with Annette, she wasn't really in the mood for gossiping today.

Barbara became aware, not for the first time today, of a loud boomy voice shouting:

'Get me off this bloody car and away from that bloody woman'

As Barbara neared the back of her car, she could not have been more unprepared for the sight that met her.

There, somehow latched onto her tow bar (the first thing as it happened ever to be attached) was the man from the community centre.

He was, after being towed, very red-faced and she could see that the back of his wheelchair had caught in the neck of her tow bar. This must have happened when she reversed.

Seeing Barbara, the man threw his arms down onto the arms of the wheelchair and sprung up to his feet. His slightly portly frame swayed in the wind as he began struggling to express his feelings.

Annette let out a yelp of surprise and Barbara decided that now might be a good time to use her "I'm feeling faint" act. She often used this when she took her car for a service. It usually ensured prompt attention and a free lift home.

On this occasion, her superb acting did not receive the accolade it so richly deserved. She wondered if she would have to go all the way with this man and drop to the floor pretending to faint. Luckily, Lionel was on hand and steadied her.

Events were starting to overpower Lionel and he too started to sway, he was also looking rather faint. After 60 years of service to the church, he had never witnessed a miracle, but what had just played out before his very eyes was indeed a true miracle. He just hoped he would remember it in the future as he was struggling more and more with his memory these days.

This man who had been wheelchair-bound was suddenly walking. He had no idea how, only that this dumpy car must have magical healing powers. Lionel couldn't help but shout out the words he had so longed to use for a lifetime.

'It's a miracle, you can walk!' he exclaimed.

'Miracle? That woman is a ruddy menace' the man shouted back, pointing at Barbara as he did so.

It was at this point that Barbara also became slightly curious about the miracle taking place on her tow bar and asked the man why he was in a wheelchair and if he could walk. The man retorted that this was none of her business and he was now in need of a jolly good stiffener to calm his nerves.

For Annette this was all too much. She could feel an overwhelming desire coming over her to spread the news of the miracle, but she was too interested in what would happen next, to leave. Torn between spreading gossip and finding more gossip she remained frozen, uttering the words:

'Oh I think you should take him inside, Barbara, for a cup of tea.' Then she turned to the man to elicit a vitally important piece of information. 'What's your name love?' she asked.

'Norman' the man replied.

'Well, Norman' said Barbara 'would you like to come in for a cup of tea or a light sherry?'

Norman grudgingly said he supposed that would be OK and with that, Annette could contain herself no longer. 'Right, I'm off,' she said, and with that she turned left - no right - no left again and hurried into her house, deciding it would be better to spread news of the miracle by telephone rather than in person. She could tell more people that way and then post something on Facebook. How she wished she'd had her smartphone with her that morning.

2. Good Planning

It had been two weeks since Barbara, had, to coin a phrase, picked up Norman. Or, as they laughingly joked, bumped into each other.

Norman had explained to Barbara he used a wheelchair to ensure attentive service at any bar and quite often a kindly soul might even buy him a drink.

He had recently moved to Welling-by-the-Sea to live with his brother, Siegfried. Unfortunately, his brother died before he arrived, and he was now left with a boat and a bungalow and no way of returning to his old life as he had been caught dipping into the till of the charity shop he worked at. The people at the shop felt sorry for him and promised not to press charges as he was moving to be with his brother who could look after him. This was a relief as Norman had already been cautioned previously for various motoring offences and attempting to sell some fake watches Siegfried had brought back for him after some of his trips abroad. Not to mention his trick of stealing his neighbour's bottles of milk before the days of people buying their dairy products in the supermarket.

Norman and Barbara kindled a friendship based on insulting each other as much as possible, but in a town where there existed no entertainment or excitement, they quickly came to rely on each other for company.

Barbara had explained to Norman, in a rare moment of confidentiality, that she dreamt of going on a luxury cruise and Norman said he would try to think of a way in which they could go.

It briefly crossed his mind that if he could find someone who could sail, they could go venture out to sea on his brother's boat. On the other hand, he could learn and impress Barbara with his nautical prowess. In the meantime, however, he'd seen a coach trip advertised at the Community Centre and would Barbara fancy a two-day antique hunting trip with an overnight stay at Trimley St. Ogthorpe?

Barbara did not fancy a two-day trip anywhere, she would rather die than be bundled onto a coach and force-fed joviality. She assumed this would include the playing of music by some cheesy entertainer from the past and a subsequent singalong. However, to keep the peace she said she would go with him to the planning evening which was to be held at the Community Centre on Wednesday evening.

Wednesday arrived and Barbara drove herself to the Community Centre. She hoped Norman would be there as she hated arriving somewhere on her own. It was awful to not have anyone awaiting her arrival.

Walking past the disabled spaces she couldn't help but steal a look at the top of the dashboards to make sure that the cars' registered keepers were indeed entitled to use the spaces. She wondered what she would do if they weren't, would she report them? And to whom? She supposed it would be too much of an effort to let their tyres down and besides, they might be going on the trip with her – if she decided to go.

To Barbara's enormous relief Norman was waiting outside the Community Centre with a pint of beer in his hand.

'What would you like?' he asked

'Tea would be very nice' Barbara replied.

Norman tutted and muttered something under his breath. He'd put her down as a sherry drinker. He ordered the tea as requested and a few minutes later they were ready to go into the meeting.

The room was typical of what Barbara had come to expect of Welling-by-the-Sea. In the centre of the room were six tables placed together to create one large boardroom table. The seating provided was a mish-mash of 1970s plastic chairs, so worn it was impossible to tell what their original colour may have been. Barbara supposed they must have been brown.

The walls were covered in what looked like a pale fabric type wallpaper with vertical brown stripes, some of the paper was starting to come away in the corner. Adorning the walls were several photographs of past local dignitaries and one of the Queen on what must have been her coronation.

Barbara sighed and took a deep breath - unfortunately, this enabled her to breathe in the fragrance of the room. A mixture of cheap furniture polish and paint from a radiator that had been left on high for too long. "Terrible," she thought. "I hope our transportation is not to this standard".

Standing at the head of the table was Josie, a tall blonde-haired lady whom Barbara judged must be in her thirties but still trying to retain a vestige of teenage youthfulness.

Josie proudly wore her hair in ponytails and was dressed in complimentary pink jogging trousers and a sweatshirt.

'Right then everyone,' she screeched. 'My name is Josie, and I will be your tour guide on the trip but tonight is our planning evening and I need you to all sit-down, NOW!'

As she finished her sentence she laid her clipboard down, checked there was a seat behind her and sat down. In Josie's past life she had been a holiday camp representative and was used to practical jokes being played on her. Sitting down with a group of strangers always made her slightly nervous – in every group she led, there would always be a practical joker. Someone ready to trip her up or try and prove to the others how clever they were. She had spent last summer learning Thai Kwando and was now ready to take on anyone.

After a minute or so, the rest of the "planners" sat down around the table. Josie decided to start.

'Right, well, thank you all for coming this evening. Let's go round the table and introduce ourselves, shall we? Starting on my right, what's your name sweetheart?'

'My name is Maud, and this is my husband, George.' Maud loved nothing more than to complain. She estimated that her complaints had resulted in a monthly budget top-up of £300 a month. She complained about everything and had been banned from several local restaurants. Her favourite and most rewarding complaints were about poor service.

'I'm George,' muttered her long-suffering husband.

Barbara noted that George was about 60, balding and around 5 foot 10. He wore a sports jacket which had clearly seen better days and some trousers which were too large for him. She supposed he must use braces. He had an air of being constantly hen-pecked, this was evident in the lines on his forehead and his constantly twitching moustache. His wife on the other hand looked very domineering and bossy. She was about the same age as George and had her blonde hair in a beehive, a short sparkly blue skirt and an open-neck beige blouse, revealing her leathery lined neck. She had piercing eyes that Barbara imagined didn't miss a thing.

George looked at the lady next to him.

'Good evening everyone, I am Agatha, and this is my sister Enid,' blurted Agatha.

Agatha and Enid were elderly spinster sisters, whose parents had decided to name them after authors. Their personas loosely resembled characters from the novels of their namesakes.

People often thought they were much older than they really were, but they enjoyed this as they loved nothing better than a spot of amateur sleuthing and dreamed of the day they would be helping the local police solve a murder. They watched back-to-back detective series on TV and were currently watching the entire Morse series for the ninth time. They much preferred the traditional BBC and ITV detective series to the popular Scandi and French series now on television.

Agatha, on one occasion, found it greatly amusing to chase after a suspect shoplifter from the local supermarket. On this occasion the suspect turned out to be nothing more than someone who had taken a free pamphlet.

Flushed with what she thought was a triumph, she kept a lookout for over a year for another occurrence, unfortunately, without any success. She had almost been banned from shopping in the store after trying to perform a citizen's arrest on a pregnant lady who was merely trying to adjust her clothing so that her bump felt more comfortable. Agatha had assumed the bump was fake and used to disguise a stolen tin of Quality Street.

Enid had pointed out that the prices were too cheap to bother with shoplifting and they should instead turn their attention to Waitrose. Sadly, their pensions didn't stretch that far. So they continued shopping in their budget supermarket with one eye on prices and the other on suspected misfits.

In their younger years, they had both wanted to be nuns. Unfortunately for reasons unknown to them they weren't accepted. However, that didn't stop them from continuing to dream of being either detectives or nuns. Sometimes, if they were bored, they would dress up as nuns and go for a cycle ride into town. Both their cycles had wicker baskets on the front. This way they could do most of their shopping and cycle home to bemused glances, their groceries hanging out of their baskets.

'Hi, yah, hi everyone, yup, um I'm er Jonathon and this is Jayne.'

Jonathon and Jayne were recent additions to the seaside town. The golf, tennis, sailing, cricket, rugby, football and croquet clubs had drawn them to Welling-by-the-Sea.

Jonathon and Jayne were very active people, both having been sports teachers before they took early retirement as a result of a generous legacy left to them by Jayne's Aunt Margaret. In their early forties, they were both still very trim and fit. They planned on buying a boat soon and had already invested in a camper van in which they intended to tour the UK. They had joined all the sports clubs in the town and had great fun purchasing suitable designer sportswear for each activity, not to mention the 10% discount they received from joining all the clubs. Like the others, they had come to the community centre hoping to meet other like-minded people.

'Thank you, Jonathon,' said Josie, 'and may I say, how very sporting you and Jayne look? I love your matching Gucci shell suits.'

Jonathon's shell suit was blue and Jaynes a complimentary pink.

'Thank you,' replied Jayne, 'we got these at Selfridges. I can highly recommend them for comfort.'

'Now, who do we have in this corner?' Josie said looking at Reginald and Diane.

Reginald was dressed quite smartly in his work suit. Barbara thought he looked as if he should have a bowler hat to finish off his outfit. He was, she imagined, in his mid-fifties but looked older, probably because he had grown his greying hair on one side of his scalp to cover his bald patch. Reginald was much taller than his wife who, at five foot, looked very demure and unsure of herself, She was blonde, slim and portrayed a wholesome, youthful appearance. However, her dress sense could have been straight out of a 1950s "how to be a housewife" book. She was wearing a red and yellow floral dress, pink high heel shoes and a soft pink cashmere cardigan. She had removed her head scarf before coming into the room.

'Shall I answer?' Diane asked Reginald.

'I don't mind,' Reginald replied, 'go ahead if you like?'

'I don't mind if you want to, or I can but, only if you don't want to?' she countered.

'Oh, for goodness sake, This is my wife Diane and I am Reginald.'

Reginald worked at Fortescue's as a Risk Assessor. He had already weighed up how long it would be before the chair Josie was sitting on would collapse under her weight. It was quite clear to him that the corner welds were not up to the job and the way she transferred her weight to the back cushion, well, that was just a lawsuit waiting to happen.

He smiled to himself, glad that he had nothing to do with local councils. Diane, his wife, could never make her mind up about anything. On the day of their wedding, Reginald had been weighing up whether to risk going to the church in his old car or if he should get a lift with his relatives.

Diane, meanwhile, couldn't decide if she should get married or wait for someone better. Her mother had pointed out that Reginald had a good job and working at Fortescue's it would not be long before they were putting a deposit down on a house in the new estate on the edge of town.

She spent so long making her mind up that on the day of her wedding, she ended up at the altar in a haze. She meant to reply 'I need a minute' but instead replied:

'I, er, er, er, er.'

Lionel, who was the vicar at the time was not only forgetful but slightly deaf. He asked her to speak up as he had a funeral in 30 minutes. What on earth was wrong with this woman?

The best man tried to ask Diane, 'Do you need more time?' but he was nervous himself and his sentence did not come out properly. Lionel heard 'I' from Diane and 'Do' from the best man and that was it, the deed was done and they were married.

Jocasta and Marcus were the last couple to introduce themselves, however, Jocasta just gave Josie a nod. Barbara thought this was rather rude of her. Jocasta looked like she was in her early 50s, she was tall, much taller than her husband. Barbara imagined she must be between six foot and six feet two inches. She had shoulder length brown hair, brown eyes and very smooth skin. Jocasta was wearing a rather expensive looking tweed trouser suit making her look very elegant. Marcus, also looked as if he was in his 50's, his hair only just starting to grey at the sides and swept back over his head. He was dressed rather conservatively wearing grey trousers, blue shirt, a striped tie and a blazer.

'Ah, Mr and Mrs Potterton-Smythe, so glad you could join us' Josie said in her poshest accent.

The Potterton-Smythe's were local shopping legends. If you needed to buy anything at all, it was best to ask Jocasta and Marcus's opinion, their commercial knowledge and expertise exceeded that of any online buyer reviews. It did not matter what it was, they knew the best model to get and where to get it for the best price. The Potterton-Smythe's were also extremely houseproud, they had the latest and best technology. They slavishly followed trends, in fact so perfect was their house that it was too good for visitors. They much preferred going to other people's houses so they could tell them about theirs. Today, however, they were hoping to get a good deal on a weekend trip.

'Now, let's get down to business' Josie announced. She went on to explain the coach they were hiring would accommodate 28 passengers, but because people may want to buy antiques, they were only half-filling it. This would allow lots of room for purchases, something which made the Potterton-Smythes look up from pouring their tea. They would be stopping at Fornlea Barn, one of the largest antiques, and bric-a-brac establishments in the UK before arriving in Trimley St. Ogthorpe for their overnight stay, then call in at Whittle St. Mary on the way back. Whittle St, Mary was a well-known town with a picturesque high street used in many TV programmes. It also featured a variety of shops, including art deco vintage which, Josie, was particularly interested in. She really wanted to buy an art deco cheese dish like her grandmother used to have.

Sid would be their driver. Sid was short for a man, about 5 foot, he had a very lined face with curly grey hair on top. He looked much older than his sixty-eight years. Barbara hoped his feet would reach the pedals of the coach.

Sid said hello to everyone squinting at their faces

'Nah, don't you worry 'bout me eyes,' he said. 'I'll have me new specs by the time we go.'

He coughed, grabbed his walking stick, and reached for another cup of tea.

Josie wanted to explain that Sid was the only driver they could get who was prepared to do the journey for the price they wanted to pay, but thought better of it.

'So, any questions?' Josie concluded.

'Yes,' said Barbara 'Are our lunches and dinner included?'

She was quickly followed by Diane.

'What if we change our minds? Do we get a refund?'

And Maud finished with, 'How do we know it will be any good?'

Josie assured them apart from anything they wished to buy, the trip was fully inclusive. Apart, that was, from alcoholic beverages – just like on the cruise ships. There were no refunds (the cheek of it!). She concluded that she had run a similar tour last year and everyone had been very satisfied. She neglected to mention that the people on last year's day trip were taken to the seaside for the day and not allowed into any shops. Many had spent the whole trip complaining about their ankle monitors chaffing. They were only too pleased to be back in remand.

And so, after everyone had paid up they were almost ready to go. All that remained was for Josie to wish everyone a good night and remind them to meet outside the chip shop on High Road North at 9.30 next Tuesday morning.

3. The Coach Trip

Sid climbed into the coach. It was going to be a long day and his wife had made him sandwiches to take with him.

'Made you some lovely egg sandwiches, your favourites. Got the eggs fresh from the butchers, Sid, and some bread from the bakers, seeing as you'll be away for a couple of days. Now you will be careful won't you? And make sure you takes them new glasses with you.'

'Yus, my love,' he replied.

It was strange being away from her after all this time. Sid had retired from coach driving 15 years ago and spent the intervening time restoring this 1960s coach. At last, he had an adventure ahead of him. Plenty of driving life left in the old dog yet, he chuckled to himself.

Sid put his glasses on. In his haste he had brought his old glasses, but he could still see perfectly well out of them. Turning the key in the ignition of his Bedford SB5, the coach fired into life, the gear lever shaking madly in anticipation of this very rare road trip.

Restoring the coach, which had belonged to his father's coach business, had been a labour of love on a very tight budget. Even now he was not sure all the parts were in the right places or indeed if he had even got the parts.

The coach coughed and spluttered until he put the choke in and then she ticked over nicely. He had filled up with diesel, checked the water, oil and tyres and was now ready to depart. Slowly the coach inched its way out of his driveway. It squeezed its way past the concrete lions that flanked his gates, standing guard over him and his good lady wife.

The five-minute drive to High Road North ensured that the engine was suitably warmed up and there were no signs of any problems.

"Well, if she managed to get this far, she should be fine," Sid thought to himself. In the past, the old coach either didn't start at all or would do hundreds of miles with no problems.

He turned into High Road North five minutes early. Outside the chip shop, he could see Josie with her clipboard and a couple dressed in jogging suits with sweat bands on their foreheads.

As he pulled up, he opened the passenger door and Josie climbed aboard.

Josie and Sid exchanged professional courtesies and then Josie turned around to Jonathon and Jayne and welcomed them aboard before crossing them off the list. Jonathon and Jayne immediately bagged the two front seats for themselves. Josie informed them that she needed the front seats so she could keep an eye on everyone and use her microphone. They could however have the seats on the other side behind the driver. Whilst this wasn't ideal, Jonathon and Jayne reluctantly agreed to move.

Their tactics were simple. The seats closest to the door meant they could be first off, grab the best bargains, best hotel rooms, and avoid queuing for restrooms. Getting into your hotel room before the others, they had discovered, was particularly important as it meant you could be in your room, have a shower before the hot water runs out and then down to the bar, securing the best seats before anyone else.

Annette had promised she would drive Barbara and Norman to High Road North on the morning of the trip. Secretly she was hoping to find out if there was any further gossip regarding the relationship between Barbara and Norman.

Barbara arrived at Annette's house first and they picked up Norman five minutes later. Desperate for any gossip Annette discretely turned the key in the ignition of her Austin Metro to the number 1 position, thus cutting out the engine.

'Oh my goodness, what's happened?' she exclaimed. 'You switched the ignition off, you stupid...' boomed Norman.

'Now then Norman, that's enough of that,' cut in Barbara. Thankful for Barbara's intervention and to hide any embarrassment, but still elicit any gossip, Annette remarked to them both:

'Oh, you're like an old married couple!' her head and beady eyes darting between Barbara and Norman, hoping that something would be given away. Nothing was and they completed the rest of their journey in silence.

Barbara and Norman decided to sit next to each other on the coach as neither could bear the thought of sitting next to anyone else. Barbara had brought a flask of coffee for them and some sandwiches just in case.

She was thankful she had the foresight to pack her portable bridge game to alleviate any dull moments. She glanced at Norman and couldn't quite tell if he was enjoying himself or not. "Too early," she thought to herself, smiled, and looked out of the window for the next arrivals.

A taxi pulled up and Marcus Potterton Smythe emerged from the offside. He hastily ran around the back of the vehicle to open the door for his wife. Jocasta elegantly extended both her legs out of the taxi. Marcus thought how stylish she looked in her Chanel suit whilst Jocasta patted herself on the back for making sure Marcus remembered to wear his cravat. Marcus paid the taxi, his wife took his arm and they glided like ice skaters across to the coach.

'I am so terribly pleased you 'ave arrived,' Josie greeted them before showing them their seats. Jocasta was pleased that the seats in front of them were empty as this would mean if they bought anything valuable, they could keep an eye on it.

'Come on Agatha or we'll be late,' goaded Enid as the pair rounded the corner and arrived at the bus. They had walked from their home ten minutes away. Agatha had insisted on walking as she wanted to take in the morning air. Enid was not so sure but was the faster on her feet. Josie ushered them in, unsure if they were going to make the entire journey and made a mental note to check the credit on her phone in case she needed to call for help.

Maud and George arrived next. Maud had wanted to arrive first at the coach, but George had been too slow getting ready, as usual. They too had walked but George was slow because he was breaking in new shoes.

'George! Will you hurry up,' shouted Maud.

'These cases are too heavy' he cried.

'Well put your back into it. Are you a man or a mouse? – no don't answer that, I think I know the answer,' retorted Maud, rather unkindly in Josie's opinion who suddenly felt sorry for George as she saw them coming up the road.

Josie got off the bus to help George with the cases. She rather liked him, he reminded her of a favourite uncle.

'Oh, don't help me, help him!' Maud remarked. 'Here's me with my lumbago and not a bit of assistance! I'll find my own way, dear!'

And with that, Maud got on the bus and sat in the spare seats in front of the Potterton-Smythes.

George eventually got on board, after watching Josie load his cases into the hold. His moustache had twitched excitedly as she heaved the cases in It was after the last one went in that he caught sight of Maud looking disapprovingly at him from above, her lips pursed in a way he knew so well. Next, her arm would be in the air. He wiped his brow and hurried to sit next to his wife.

''Bout time' she welcomed him with.

Jocasta thought she ought to point out that there were plenty more free seats on the coach but looking at Maud's crimplene dress and general demeanour she decided she had better keep quiet and ask Josie at a suitable moment to relocate them. Maud and George, she assumed to be very much a part of the lower orders.

Last to arrive were Reginald and Diane. Reginald had been checking their house insurance to make sure anything they took with them was suitably covered and Diane was having last-minute second thoughts. She was, after all, about to board a bus with a load of strangers. What if they were awful people? What if she didn't get on with them? There were a hundred other things she could be doing instead of going on this trip.

If only she could make her mind up. Before she knew it Reginald had got them on the bus to High Road North and they were outside the coach.

Josie was exhausted from loading cases. Sid had said his back was playing him up, so she left Reginald to load his own cases, deciding that either Sid makes a miraculous recovery or each passenger henceforth can load and unload their own cases! She couldn't however fail to notice the two belts wrapped around each of Reginald and Diane's suitcases, she assumed this was for extra security.

With Reginald and Diane safely on board and the time now approaching ten thirty, it was time to depart. It had taken an hour for everyone to arrive and get everything loaded into the coach. This was much longer than she had planned for.

Sid restarted the Coach and then felt a tap on his arm as Josie reminded him that she needed to make some announcements before they could depart.

'Good morning everyone and welcome aboard. We shall in a moment be starting our Antiquing adventure. But first some housekeeping.'

'Housekeeping?' Agatha ventured to her sister.

'Yes, dear it's so that we know what's happening,' replied Enid. Agatha nodded but couldn't quite get what she meant. Housekeeping in her day was akin to housework and this was meant to be a break away from it all.

Josie proceeded to explain the schedule and what to do in an emergency. When she had finished, she asked if there were any questions and was pleased to note there were none. Sid then fired up the old coach, let out the clutch and they were off.

Their first destination was to be Fornlea Barn, an Antiques Emporium in Frappington Horsley. This was about seventy-five miles away and would take them about two hours if the traffic was light.

The old coach ran quite well through the countryside, its occupants taking comfort in the drone of the vintage engine and the warmth of direct sunlight through the un-tinted windows.

Sid was delighted that the meters for oil pressure, voltage charge and water temperature remained healthy. Looking at his watch it was now eleven thirty and there was another hour to go before they would arrive at their first stop and their lunch. He eyed up the sandwiches his wife had made earlier, they were on the shelf wrapped in paper inside the Tupperware sandwich container. It wouldn't do any harm to have one, he thought.

Gingerly he managed to get the lid off the container. The sun had warmed the sandwiches up beautifully, but he didn't particularly want warm egg sandwiches.

Eating egg sandwiches in a confined public space is not the most endearing social activity one can indulge in at the best of times. On a hot day in a vintage coach it was most definitely not the best of things to do, no matter how hungry you are.

'Ere, what's that smell? Oh it stinks!' shouted Josie, into the microphone she had forgotten to turn off.

'It's me lunch and very nice it is too,' replied Sid.

'Eating whilst driving a coach is really not something I think you should be doing,' advised Reginald, 'in fact I would very much advise you desist from the activity. I am almost certain that it will invalidate your insurance,' he went on to advise.

Sid didn't seem to care, he was enjoying his sandwich too much. So much so, in fact, that a combination of his old glasses and the distraction of the sandwich made him miss his turn. The intensity of the smell of Sid's sandwiches got worse and Josie asked him again to put the lid on the box and wait till they stopped to eat. Sid ignored her. Each piece of sandwich rolled around his open mouth like the contents of a cement mixer. Josie noticed that some of the passengers were starting to make uncomfortable groaning noises.

Maud thought it absolutely disgusting that their driver should be seen eating and Jocasta said this would never happen if they had paid more for a reputable company rather than Sid and his restored coach.

Maud turned to her husband and demanded that he do something about the driver.

'What can I do?' he protested but proceeded to elevate himself out of his seat and into the aisle.

'Josie, my dear, can you ask the driver to err, umm...' he started to say but was distracted by Josie's attempts to get out of her seat. By missing the turn the coach was now on quite a rough road with everyone being jostled around. The microphone had dropped into Josie's lap and was making crunching noises through the speakers.

'What's going on up there George? What are you doing to her?' shouted Maud above the noise.

Sid continued to eat his sandwich and seeing the coach approach a Ford, decided to hit the brakes. This was enough to topple George across Josie's lap, his legs and feet sticking out into the aisle. Josie's microphone continued to report the carnage at the front of the bus.

Jonathon decided he needed to help and got up to try and rescue George. Unfortunately, he too got caught out by the force of the braking coach and ended up across Sid. Sid, panicking, tried to push Jonathon off him so that he could see where he was going. Instead of grabbing Jonathon's arm, he pulled the door release lever and just as the coach shuddered to a stop his sandwich fell to the floor. Jonathon slipped on the eggy mess and was catapulted out of the door and into a watery ford.

The coach had now stopped. George managed to get himself upright and Josie stood up ready to take command of the situation.

'You idiot!' shouted Jonathon. 'Look what you've done to my clothes.'

Jayne got off the bus to help her husband up to his feet and back onto the coach. Luckily it was only his tracksuit bottoms that were soaked. He was able to take them off and sit in his boxer shorts whilst they dried.

Josie asked everyone to remain calm over the intercom whilst giving Sid a thoroughly reproachful glance. She was angry, of that there was no doubt.

'Sid, do you know where we are?' she asked.

'Sort of, at least I did until I turned off the main road,' he replied.

'In other words: we are lost!' came the exasperated conclusion.

Then, in Josie's opinion, the holy gods of the Bluewater shopping centre must have taken pity on her, for the idea came into her head that what they needed was a Tom Tom, a satellite navigation device!

She knew she didn't have one and she was 99.999% certain that Sid wouldn't have one.

'Does anyone have a satellite navigation device?' she asked over the intercom. Sid immediately responded

'I don't need one of them things, I've got me sense of direction and me eyes.'

Josie ignored him and asked again.

'Please, does anyone have a satellite navigation device?'

Jocasta stood up and replied, Well, I don't know if it's any good, but I have something on my phone that shows me how to get to Brent Cross?'

'Brent Cross?' piped up Norman. 'We're nowhere near bloody Brent Cross.'

Barbara told him to be quiet as that wasn't the point.

Jocasta spoke into her phone and asked it to calculate the route to Fornlea Barn, Frappington Horsley. After three seconds it had calculated the route. They were only 51.5 miles away and their ETA would be two o'clock by the fastest route. Jocasta handed the phone to Josie so that she could pass on the spoken instructions to Sid.

Sid started the engine, put the bus into 3rd gear to get some traction and slowly eased his way out of the water. He had seen this done in many films. If it did not work, he would have to let the tyres down to get more grip. Luckily the old coach responded, and they were back on their way with Josie echoing directions from the phone to Sid.

Life inside the bus returned to normal. Jonathan's tracksuit bottoms dried so he was able to put them back on and Agatha and Enid handed out some of the sandwiches they had made. More egg sandwiches graced the inside of the coach. The sisters had agreed before leaving that it was better to bring too much food than not enough and to always be prepared. The baggage containing their nun's outfits was a case in point, however, both were secretly pleased that they brought it with them. Should the opportunity arise, they could dress up as nuns.

Josie continued to echo directions to Sid, 'Left. Right. Join the M1'.

'Join the M1? Are you sure?' questioned Sid.

'Yes, just do what I say,' came the reply.

Barbara was starting to get anxious now, she had nodded off and awoke unsure as to where they were. It was two thirty and they seemed to be stuck in a traffic jam on what looked like a motorway. She got up and went to the front of the coach and asked Josie,

'Are you sure this is the right way? I mean we seem to be on a motorway and there isn't one anywhere near Frappington Horsley. We should be on "A" roads.'

'Told you this weren't right,' piped up Sid.

'Well don't ask me,' replied Josie, 'Jocasta put the details in.'

Hearing the conversation Marcus went to the front of the coach and decided to check Jocasta's phone. His amiable expression soon changed to one of exasperation.

Jocasta was a bit of a technophobe; she didn't like technology unless it carried a premium price tag and she didn't really spend any time learning how to use it properly. She was more than capable, just not interested.

'Ahem, I think what's happened here is that Jocasta's phone is pre-programmed with two destinations, Brent Cross and home. Unfortunately, it didn't understand Frappington Horsley and defaulted to Brent Cross. On the upside, it didn't take us home but on the downside, we are ten miles from Brent Cross!'

Trying hard to save face, Marcus set the route to Fornlea Barn. It now looked as if they wouldn't get there until at least five o'clock, assuming they could get off the motorway and turn round. Josie asked him to try the route to the hotel instead, after all they had paid for it and she could rearrange things so that they had a good evening and then did some more antiquing tomorrow instead.

Marcus informed her that they were approximately three hours away, some 130 miles, almost right back where they had started from!

An executive decision was taken by Josie to head for the hotel. They should be there by six thirty. She duly informed everyone on the coach of the change in plans and thanked Barbara and Marcus for their help. After all, it wasn't her fault they had got lost, Jocasta had entered the wrong details!

As darkness fell, much to everyone's relief - not least Sid, who by now was starting to regret not going back for his glasses - the Coach pulled into the hotel car park.

Jonathon and Jayne had primed themselves for the off. With the stakes so high it was imperative that they were ready to go as soon as the door opened, if not before. They had praised themselves for having the foresight to grab seats as close to the front of the coach as they could. Those hot showers were waiting for them, and they would be the first into the dining room.

Jocasta meanwhile had been pondering whom they should sit next to at dinner for the past 15 miles. She eventually reached the conclusion that Agatha and Enid would be the best company. They must have an inordinate number of stories to tell and their undeniable longevity may mean that might even know a thing or two about Antiques.

Agatha and Enid meanwhile were each thinking it had been a long day and they wanted nothing better than to chill out and relax in their nun outfits.

Josie asked people to leave the coach starting with people at the front so that there wouldn't be a scramble,

'Don't worry about your bags, Sid will see they are with you once you are in the hotel'

Sid grunted at the prospect and proceeded to get out of the coach and start loading the luggage onto his trolley.

Josie strode into the reception area; this was the bit she liked best. The feeling of being in control and in charge. Rooms sorted she handed out the keys to everyone, apart from Jonathon and Jayne who had already grabbed theirs from the receptionist. Josie asked everyone to meet again in reception in half an hour so they could have dinner together.

The restaurant took the last orders at nine o'clock and it was already seven o'clock.

4 The Overnight Stay

Almost to Barbara's relief, Norman had been allocated the room next to hers. She supposed this was a good thing as she had grown to feel safer with him close by.

Maud and George had the room opposite. Theirs was a family room with both a double bed and two single beds.

Maud immediately started checking for signs of dust and pubic hair in the bathroom. She regularly watched the program *Four in a Bed* and knew that if the room didn't pass her stringent testing, she could ask for another one. The top of the pictures were OK, no dust there, under the bed seemed good too and the sheets were crisp and clean. She supposed it would have to do.

Their luggage arrived shortly afterwards, and George insisted on having pre-dinner drinks in their room from a secret supply of whisky he had smuggled in his luggage.

Agatha and Enid were also settling into their room, pleased that their luggage had arrived. Enid had packed everything into a Samsonite case a concerned nephew had given them.

He had doubts that their 1950s cases would stand up to any more travels.

Agatha threw back the lid and was rather surprised to see that their nuns' outfits seemed to have grown hoods. In fact, they looked totally different, what on earth was Whey Protein? Enid suggested that they get changed anyway into the black outfits as they looked extremely comfortable, and she didn't have anything else to get changed into.

Besides if they were lucky, they could get to keep them as someone most likely wouldn't want them back after they had worn them and extolled the virtues of their comfort. So, the two sisters got changed, laughing at each other with their hoodies. Agatha remarked that she hoped it was a buffet dinner as she could load up her plate with her hood up and not be recognised. Enid commented that she rather thought that was why people loved wearing hoodies. They wondered why blazoned across the front of their hoodies was the word Guess.

'Perhaps people are meant to guess what religion we are?' Enid asked of her sister.

'Just say we are considering,' she replied.

All was not well in Jonathon and Jayne's room; their Samsonite case had also arrived and Jayne was impatient to get changed and go down to dinner.

She scolded Jonathon for forgetting to pack their protein drinks, she was sure she would end up putting on a few pounds, and worst still the black tracksuits Jonathon had bought as a surprise were surprisingly heavy and not at all what she had imagined. He'd said it was a surprise!

Jonathon realised something was wrong and these were not the clothes he had packed. Rather sheepishly he explained that there was a possibility they had someone else's suitcase.

As they had no other clothes they decided to put on the outfits. Jonathon's just about fitted. When they looked in the mirror, they couldn't help but laugh and wonder who on earth the suitcase could belong to as they had no nuns in their company. Eventually, the pair made their way down to the restaurant.

Josie had arranged one big table for them all to sit at and most people were already seated by the time Jonathon and Jayne arrived.

Josie sniggered and spat half her gin and tonic out at the sight of the pair in the Nun's outfits.

"That's all we need - a couple of weirdos," she thought. Agatha and Enid clocked their outfits but said nothing, for the moment. They were enjoying themselves. Unfortunately for the sisters, Jonathon recognised the outfits they were wearing and decided to sit next to them. He figured he could have a word with them later and sort the mess out.

Choices for dinner were rather limited, one meat dish and one vegetarian dish. Of course, that was not going to please Maud, she had been looking forward to a weekend of gastronomic delights, fine dining, sophisticated conversation and being bought something special by George. It didn't look like this was going to happen. Nearly everyone opted for the

Chicken Casserole since the vegetarian dish was, rather predictably, salad.

After dinner, everyone retired to the resident's lounge and Jonathan took the opportunity to speak to Agatha and Enid. Both parties agreed that their outfits would look better on the other couple and so they decided that as soon as they got back to their rooms, they would swap the cases.

From the reception desk they could hear a rather loud and angry exchange of words

'What do you mean you ain't got a room for me?' bellowed Sid,

'I'm sorry sir but we just don't have a booking in your name. We can accommodate you tomorrow, just not tonight,' the receptionist was trying to explain.

Josie realised that in her attempt at being efficient, she had booked a room for everyone apart from the driver. This she put down to having booked the rooms so that they married up to the number of seats being taken on the bus.

Josie attempted to pacify Sid.

'Look Sid, you could always sleep on your coach, I'm sure it's very comfortable.'

'There's no way, I'm sleeping on that coach tonight, it's cold for one thing – how's about you sleep on the coach and I take your bed?' Sid offered.

George couldn't help but overhear the heated exchange and put forward a third proposal.

'Look,' he said, 'we have a room with a spare bed in it, why don't you have that? To be honest, Maud might stop complaining for five minutes.'

'Spare bed in your room?' Sid repeated. 'ere, you're not into anyfing funny are yer? Cost I ain't that sort of man, I'm 'appily married, if you know what I mean.'

'Of course, not,' replied George, 'I was just trying to help you out.'

Reluctantly Sid agreed and thanked George.

'Betty, where's my Warninks Advocaat?' shouted a rather overweight grey-haired old lady as she swept into the lounge 'I will not sit down without my drink'.

'I was just about to go and get it, please have some patience' replied a rather flustered Betty. Betty was a rather short stubby lady in her early seventies. She liked to dress as if she were a pensioner in the nineteen sixties, her mostly greying hair she wore in a bun purely for the low maintenance aspect.

'Who are you lot?' asked the overweight grey-haired old lady of the lounge occupants.

'Well, we are staying here tonight as we are on an antique-buying trip' replied Barbara on behalf of the group. 'Who are you and what, may I ask, brings you here?'

'My name is Gwyneth-Anne and I'm here with my friend and driver Betty. We are looking for houses in the area.'

The reality was that Gywneth-Anne and Betty drove all over the country whenever they had the opportunity to take a holiday. Their intention was to stay in a nice hotel and then spend the day looking at houses that had 'for sale' signs up.

They would pretend to the vendors that they were interested and would speak to the Agents in the morning, but could they have a quick look around as they were here now? It seemed a shame to wait another day when they were so keen.

Most people didn't even question their motives and it wouldn't be long before they were shown around and then invited to tea and cake or biscuits. If they were extremely lucky, they may even get a meal and save themselves from having to pay for dinner. This gave them the opportunity to later recount endless tales of house hunting and how perfect their own small town was.

George, in an attempt to take Maud's mind off their overnight guest, looked at the Juke Box in the corner of the room. He hadn't seen one of these for years and looking at the single records contained within it, the selection had remained untouched since it was new.

He was reminded of the times he and Maud would dance together in the coffee bar when they were younger. "Oh, why not?", he thought as he put his 20-pence piece into the machine. He looked at the card displaying the songs but couldn't quite make out the numbers, In the end, he decided to choose something at random. One, two, eight, sounded like a lucky number to him. The machine lit up and a single was plopped onto the platter, then an arm lowered gently onto its vinyl surface.

The volume must have been stuck because the loud clicks and surface noise had everyone looking at the open fire in case it had gotten out of control. But no, it was the jukebox.

'At break of day,' boomed out Tom Jones.

'Oh it's my favourite song ever, Delilah,' shrieked Gwyneth Anne. Being of Welsh extraction she unequivocally adored Tom Jones.

Betty and Gwyneth lived in separate houses on the Welsh border, they had often heard his songs in the pubs and hotels nearby.

The snowball must have been laced with something as soon Gwyneth Anne was up on her feet swinging away to the song to a bewildered audience.

She made her way towards Sid who, not unsurprisingly took a step backwards. It was the Piano behind him she was after and she sat down at it just in time for the chorus.

Her hand rising and crashing down on the keyboard she soon picked up the rhythm and was starting to enjoy herself. She thanked her lucky stars she had been taught to play by ear.

Norman found her rather amusing; she was in fact just his sort of woman. A splendid frame, a good sense of humour and a marvellous entertainer. He found himself wandering over and joining in with the singing.

Soon the whole party had thrown caution to the wind and joined Gwyneth Anne at the piano.

As the record ended Gywneth moved on to playing 'the green green grass of home' and then several other hits of the nineteen sixties. She hadn't had so much fun in years.

Josie was reminded of her time as a holiday rep in Spain – she'd never failed to be surprised at how young and old holidaymakers always knew the words to Delilah and Sweet Caroline after a few drinks.

By now the time was getting very late and they all decided it was now time for bed. Norman felt rather sorry that Gwyneth Anne and Betty wouldn't be joining them the next day. Barbara was secretly relieved.

'I must see Barbara,' a rather shaky voice could be heard from reception. 'I really must see her, it's terribly important .'

Lionel the vicar had arrived at the end of their evening.

'Lionel, what on earth are you doing here?' asked Barbara.

'I simply had to come,' replied Lionel.

'Well, what is it? What on earth has happened?' Barbara asked.

'That's the thing, I can't remember now. I left the house and caught a train here and then a taxi and it's been so terribly draining I've completely forgotten why I had to come and see you. Oh darn it.'

Poor Lionel had completely forgotten what was so important and now it was too late to go home.

Jonathon put an arm around him to calm him down. Lionel looked at him and could feel his temper rising.

'Why are you dressed in a nun's outfit?' he asked Jonathon.

'Ahh erm yes, that, well, you see our cases got mixed up and to tell you the truth I'm quite enjoying being in something other than a tracksuit.'

'Enjoying it! Enjoying it!' screamed Lionel at him. He really would never understand young people. Gosh, he needed a sit-down and some water. What on earth was he going to do now, where would he stay?

It was Maud's turn for yet another good deed. She offered Lionel the remaining spare bed in her room. Lionel accepted the kind offer, not realising he would be sharing with three other people. He hoped that by the morning he would remember what it was he had to tell Barbara. Everyone then made their way up to their rooms for the night.

The owners of Bressingfield Manor descended from a Scottish Highlands Clan and had long ago decided that there were some traditions their guests south of the border would benefit from. This came in the form of playing the bagpipes at seven in the morning in place of an alarm call.

The bagpipe player had long since gone. Wee Shuggie had had enough of the insults and things being thrown at him from angry guests at their windows.

Instead of live music, they piped The Royal Scott's Dragoon Guards' greatest hits through the hotel's speaker system. The playing of this rather remarkable CD every morning ensured nearly everyone came down to breakfast at the same time.

For Maud this was the final straw. Not only had she had to put up with George, Sid and Lionel's snoring, she had hardly slept and to make matters worse, when she tried to find a bathroom to sleep in, she witnessed Jonathon taking his case to the room with the old ladies.

She couldn't help but put her ear to the old ladies door after he went in. Although she couldn't hear much, she decided that he must be a very strange man. She'd heard his laugh getting louder and louder and then stop. She figured he must be approaching the door. Fortunately, she managed to get back into her own room before he could see her.

Norman heard the bagpipes first; he had knocked the speaker off the wall and onto his bedside table in his attempt at swatting a fly.

'Christ!' he bellowed. 'What the hell is that?'

It sounded like it was in his head.

'Stop that infernal bloody noise,' he shouted.

The noise continued as he went out into the hallway and repeated his command. This time everyone else came out to see what the problem was and who was playing the bagpipes.

Barbara started laughing when she caught sight of Norman. Instead of pyjamas and a dressing gown, he appeared to have what she could only describe as a poncho.

'What do you look like and what are you wearing?'

'Oh this, this is what is called an oodie, I was given it for Christmas by one of my nieces, and I have to say I quite like it. Jolly comfortable.'

The sight of Norman in his "oodie" calmed the mood and the bagpipe CD eventually stopped playing.

Half an hour later everyone was seated ready for their breakfasts. Josie was pleased to note that all their suitcases were in the hall ready to be collected and loaded onto the coach - a job that poor Sid had had to do before being allowed to tuck into his bacon roll.

Once everyone had finished breakfast and they were boarded onto the coach, Josie took the microphone in her hand and explained that the new itinerary would be to miss out Fornlea Bar and go instead to Whittle St. Mary. She explained that Whittle St. Mary was crammed full of antique shops, and they would have plenty of time to explore. She had booked them in for lunch at a nineteen-forties-themed tearoom. All being well they should be back in Welling-by-the-Sea around ten o'clock that evening.

5. Antiquing

Sid started the coach and they were soon on their way.

The trip to Whittle St. Mary proved largely uneventful. Jocasta moaned that she didn't feel particularly lively this morning as the hotel didn't have any fresh coffee. It only had instant which she never touched as it gave her a migraine.

Agatha and Enid were very pleased with themselves. They had managed to change into their nuns outfits, this they felt sure would play a major part in securing suitably rewarding discounts in their Antiquing.

Agatha was after a small silver hip flask as she often craved a very small sherry when they were doing the monthly food shop. A hip flask would provide just the boost she needed to carry on and finish what had to be the most boring task ever invented. She often mused that she would rather stick her fingers into a live light bulb socket than go shopping. However, just like Barbara, she thought it was fun to see if there were any bargains to be had in the yellow-label aisle.

Agatha had worked for the Home Office in London. She pretended her job was far more dangerous than it really was and for excitement had joined the London Ladies Clay Pigeon Shooting Club. So good was she at the sport that she once won the national championships. Enid meanwhile had stayed at home looking after their parents and worrying about her brave sister. Once their parents had passed and Agatha retired, Enid decided they should move to Welling-by-the-Sea. Agatha reluctantly agreed.

Jonathan and Jayne looked trendy in their Guess jogging suits. Jonathan was looking forward to exploring the village and hoped Jayne didn't find it too boring. Jayne loved excitement. Unfortunately, Welling-by-the-Sea failed to deliver on that count. It hadn't turned out to be the retirement they had hoped for, but it was early days, and they were enjoying spending time with their newfound friends.

Lionel was gripping his pocket watch trying for the life of him to remember what he had come to tell Barbara. He just couldn't remember. He supposed it can't have been that important, but then again would he have travelled all this way for nothing?

Barbara told him not to worry, whatever it could be could wait until they got home. Perhaps he should just relax and enjoy the trip.

It was only Norman that was unhappy. This wasn't really his sort of thing and Barbara was being nice enough towards him but a little frosty. Was this her way? Was she like this to every man she met? Maybe he was just being silly?

Anyway, he would enjoy the antiques and might even buy something. He fancied a pair of antique oars which he could hang up on his wall. They would provide great protection in the event of a break-in and be a talking point as he could say they were taken from an old boat of his, thus giving credibility to his nautical ambitions. Yes, that's what he would buy if he could find any.

Reginald and Diane were the only two who had decided not to buy anything and only look. Reginald had said that if they bought any furniture, it might be riddled with woodworm and Diane was against buying anything in case it wasn't worth what they'd paid for it. For these two this was a fact-finding mission as they had booked a similar trip to France the next year.

Just outside Paris there is a huge flea market and they were looking forward to going on that trip.

The coach eventually pulled up outside The Hangmans Inne in Whittle St., Mary. The High Street was around a mile and a half long and full of period buildings, every third or fourth shop seemed to be an antique or bric-a-brac shop.

This was truly a shopper's dream and Jocasta, and Marcus couldn't wait to start shopping. Jocasta knew that if they could get something at the right price then it was worth having it shipped home and that someone local would do it for the right fee. Buying too much had never bothered her as where there was a will there was a way.

Josie hardly had time to remind everyone to meet back at the coach at one o'clock for lunch. She just about managed to get the words out as everyone scrambled for the door once it was open. Anyone watching would have thought the coach was on fire. The speed with which the first people off the coach started racing up the high street would have made Dale Winton proud.

Barbara and Norman were the last to leave the coach. Barbara wasn't particularly bothered if she bought anything or not and Norman didn't mind too much if he didn't find any oars, so long as he had some quality time with Barbara.

Lionel was waiting for them outside the coach. He still couldn't remember what it was he needed to tell Barbara, but he knew it would come to him sooner or later.

Barbara asked Lionel, much to Norman's annoyance, if he would like to join them on their excursion, to which he agreed.

The first shop they came across was an art deco shop. As they walked in, they were acutely aware of being watched by a black-haired woman of around 60. She did not appear to trust them,

"Goodness knows why," thought Barbara, "I mean it isn't as if we are hooligans."

'Are you looking for anyfing in pawticular?' asked the shopkeeper, secretly wishing she had remembered to put her teeth in before serving these customers.

'No' replied Barbara 'I'm just after something interesting as a memento of today's visit.'

'Well, we are a specialist shop, I doubt you will find a memento in here, our regular customers, of course, are discerning collectors of art deco, and I shwhould add it's quite expensive. Most of them telephone us to see if we can get objects in for them. Would you like our number?'

Lionel looked at the shopkeeper and then Barbara – he remembered why he had to see Barbara! Turning towards her, he said,

'Come outside, I need to speak to you on a matter of the utmost urgency. I've remembered why I needed to talk to you!'

Barbara was only too pleased to leave the shop. What a nasty little woman, and so rude! She doubted her shop did very well at all! Norman dutifully followed Barbara.

Outside the shop Lionel was most animated. Barbara thought he was on the verge of a heart attack, his face was so red.

'Now, I had a call from Elsie last week. You remember Elsie, don't you? She was the lady who used to clean for me. She left in a hurry, something to do with a letter from the inland revenue. Anyway, when she left, she forgot her ring and I said I would keep it safe for her should she choose to collect it at some point. Well, she has decided to collect it.'

He looked relieved now that he had remembered what it was that he needed to see Barbara about. Norman asked Lionel why it was a problem. Surely, he still had the ring? Unfortunately, as with most things to do with Lionel it was not straightforward or a simple matter of handing the ring back.

So fond was Lionel of Elsie, that for a while he carried the ring around with him.   That was until he married Ben and Lucy, a young couple from the village. The night before he had been trying out some wines for the Village fete. What had started out as a chore ended up being something he very much enjoyed. So much so that he managed to get through two bottles of wine whilst playing his favourite Seekers record at full blast.

The next day when it came to marrying the couple he was rather the worse for wear and upon finding out that the best man had forgotten the ring he decided to lend them Elsie's ring since it was in his pocket. The ring was used but never returned as the couple moved to Australia in order to escape their rather overbearing in-laws.

It was a simple silver ring and he thought, maybe Barbara may have one or she could help him find one?

Norman shook his head in disbelief. Ye gods, what was wrong with these people?

Barbara patted Lionel on the arm and said he was not to worry as she was sure they would find one somewhere.

Their combined objective now was to find a small plain silver ring. The next shop they came across was in fact a bric-a-brac shop and they went straight in. Fortunately for them, the shopkeeper seemed quite friendly.

The shop was crammed with small second-hand or antique-looking objects. It was one of those old-fashioned shops that were very popular on the outskirts of large towns like

Bournemouth. Some of the contents had been there for years and they were covered in dust.

Barbara could see in one corner a stuffed animal, which she really didn't approve of and almost walked out of the shop just as Lionel exclaimed he had found a ring that looked just like the one he had given away.

Picking the ring up he asked Barbara to try it on, which she did and remarked it was a perfect fit.

The shopkeeper looked on rather perplexed. Why would a vicar be buying a second-hand ring for this lady, was he planning on marrying her? And who on earth was this other chap?

'How much is this?' asked Lionel.

'Well, I suppose I could let you have that one for, ooooh, let me think... Now the lady who brought that in was quite stylish and I paid her a fair price. Allowing for my profit - and I'm hardly making anything on this - one hundred and fifty pounds? Does that sound fair?'

Lionel nearly choked. A hundred and fifty pounds! That was way more than he had expected to pay, and the ring needed cleaning. It was very grubby.

However, it was his mistake, and it was up to him to put the mistake right. He also supposed that the poor shopkeeper needed to make a living and it wouldn't be fair to try and negotiate the price down. In fact, he was rather grateful he had managed to find a ring so close to the one he had lent Ben. He handed over his debit card and the transaction was complete in no time at all.

The shopkeeper popped the ring into a small box for him and they left the shop.

The remainder of their morning was spent looking at the other shops on the road. Norman, remembered that he had wanted his sitting room to look like a gentleman's club. He hadn't seen any oars but had seen several antiques that caught his eye, in particular a burgundy leather wing chair. The chair fitted his portly frame beautifully and it felt very comfortable. Unfortunately, the transportation costs outweighed the cost of buying the chair and he couldn't imagine that even between the three of them they could carry it all the way to the coach.

Barbara had said that if he really wanted it, they could always drive back in her car another day. The thought of going anywhere near her car after the last time he met it, didn't particularly thrill him.

Meanwhile, Marcus and Jocasta had scoured the shops and unfortunately couldn't find anything to buy. They decided that as it was nearly lunchtime they would head to the Art Deco shop they'd seen Barbara, Norman and Lionel go into earlier.

As they entered the shop the dark-haired lady gave a sigh. It was almost time for her lunch break and she wanted to shut the shop. She hoped these two wouldn't be long, however, they did look like they had deep pockets so she might be eating cod and chips for lunch instead of a fish cake and mushy peas. She must remember to get her top set of false teeth out of the cleaning solution.

She'd popped them in for a clean earlier as she'd eaten porridge for breakfast and bits of oats had got caught in them. This was her second set of customers in one day without her teeth in.

Jocasta spotted some napkin rings and she looked closely at them. They had a lovely art deco octagonal shape, but they were quite dull, although she assumed they would clean up nicely. In fact, most things on the table she was looking at were dull. She imagined charity shops were like this.

'I say, how much are these, please?'

The dark-haired lady barely looked up deciding that this couple had money and she would be better off appearing not to need a sale.

'Fwee to you' she muttered.

'Did you say "free"?' Jocasta asked for clarification.

'Yes, fwee,' came the irritated reply. What on earth was wrong with these people?

'That's jolly decent of you, thanks,' Marcus replied. And with that, they popped the rings into Jocasta's handbag and proceeded to the shop door.

'Oi, where are you going with my fings?'

'We are late for lunch but thank you for the rings,' said Jocasta grabbing the door handle.

The dark-haired shopkeeper couldn't believe her eyes – what were these two up to? She'd told them they were three hundred pounds and yet here they were committing daylight robbery in front of her very eyes. There was nothing for it but to hit the alarm button and take the shop into lockdown!

She pressed the button under the till and with that blue lights started flashing and a siren started to wail – it was an old siren originally intended to warn people of incoming luftwaffe activity. The iron grill on the front window started coming down and the dark-haired lady grabbed her air rifle, ready to take aim and hold up these nasty thieves until the napkin rings were safely back in her possession.

Marcus and Jocasta stumbled out of the shop and onto the pavement. This had to be the worst shopping experience ever. The woman inside the shop was clearly deranged.

Opposite the shop a passing police car, seeing the flashing alarm lights and hearing the air raid siren, almost, but not quite, managed a handbrake turn on the busy road.

This was PC Bobby Knolles first solo trip on patrol and he was delighted at the prospect of a full-on raid. He could see the headlines, "PC Bobby Knolles apprehends suspects in antique jewel heist."

The panda car mounted the pavement almost knocking over Jocasta and Marcus. He had them in his grasp. The door to the shop opened and out came the shopkeeper pointing her air rifle directly at Marcus and Jocasta. She did not even notice the police car.

PC Knolles ducked down and picked up the radio microphone, calling for immediate tactical response backup. He explained that he had either an armed robbery in progress or a hostage situation. Either way, he and the public were in danger.

'Hand the rings back wow!' stuttered the dark-haired shopkeeper, again wishing she had put her teeth in.

Despite everything, Jocasta was not going to hand back something that they had been told was free.

By now there was quite a crowd gathering with people taking selfies of themselves and the armed robbery going on in the background. Most people however were keeping their distance, not knowing whether the gun was real or not.

Very gingerly, but ultimately bravely, PC Knolles opened his car door and stood up.

'Mrs Brockelhurst.' He could now clearly see the dark-haired lady and remembered her name. He used to buy sweets from her on the way to school when the shop was a newsagent, and he was a child. Apart from accusing him of stealing some gobstoppers once, he knew deep down, she was a good person. 'Put the gun down and put your hands in the air where I can see them, please.'

'No, I want my fings back fwom these two fieves!' Mrs Brockelhurst's speech was getting worse the more agitated she became.

As the crowd grew bigger, Jocasta noticed that some of her new friends were in the crowd. She couldn't help but notice the sight of Agatha and Enid in full nuns regalia alongside Barbara, Norman and Lionel. The embarrassment she felt knew no limits. This was turning into the worst trip ever.

Lionel, seeing his former parishioners clearly in trouble, started to walk over – no one would shoot a vicar he decided, and with that Agatha joined him. Enid rather timidly decided to stay put with the others.

'Jocasta, dear, is everything all right?' ventured Agatha.

'Does it look like everything's all bloody right?' came the reply.

'Stay back!' shouted PC Knolles.

But they wouldn't. Lionel and Agatha joined Marcus and Jocasta on the front line.

At that moment more sirens could be heard and two rather large police vans came to an abrupt halt – the back doors burst open and out jumped ten armed police guards. The Tactical Response Unit was based only five miles up the road. This was a stroke of luck for PC Knolles.

Agatha looked at the gun. This was no armed rifle, she could tell as it had no trigger. she looked again and then inched closer. The safety catch was on too. Her time spent clay pigeon shooting was beginning to pay off. Slowly she grabbed the end of the barrel.

'Oh, dear lord,' muttered Lionel. 'What are you doing?'

'This gun isn't real,' said Agatha, 'and I am disarming the assailant.'

'That's my job,' interjected PC Knolles

Mrs Brockelhurst was not going to give up her gun easily and she pulled it back. Agatha, sensing that now would be a good time to play dirty, kicked Mrs Brockelhurst on the shin and in doing so took possession of the gun.

At last it was hers. She turned the gun round so she could hold it properly and then swung around to tell everyone they were now safe.

She was amazed to see ten armed police officers right in front of her, all of them now ducking as she swung the gun around.

To the onlookers, this was indeed a strange sight. For the second time in one day PC Knolles asked a lady to put the gun down and raise her arms in the air.

Agatha decided that now would be a good time to oblige and so she put the gun down and her arms in the air. As she did so, the hip flask she had bought earlier fell to the floor and a rather bemused Lionel wondered if it had anything in it. He did hope so.

After some intense negotiations between the right arm of the law and the left arm of the church, Jocasta handed back the napkin rings. The armed police stood down and PC Knolles returned to the Police Station to write up his report. What a day, such a shame he didn't get to arrest anyone.

Jocasta and Marcus swore they would never bother with second-hand again, they knew it had been a mistake to even bother.

'You know where you are with John Lewis' remarked Marcus to Jocasta.

6. A Hidden Gem

With the excitement over, the group made their way to the Nineteen Forties Tea Rooms for their lunch before the long drive home. Josie wondered if she shouldn't just take them to a pub. She needed a drink and was sure the others did too.

The ladies running the Tea Room were dressed in suitably period vintage dresses with pinnies over the top. The piped jazz through the speakers added to the ambience as did the old newspapers and pictures of King George VI with Winston Churchill.

A long table had been set aside for them at the back of the room and they all sat down. Sid joined them and remarked that he would have to bring his good lady wife to this place.

After all the gun action and noise of the air raid siren, it seemed fitting that they were somehow transported back to wartime Britain.

Lunch was a rather boisterous affair, Marcus and Jocasta seeing the funny side of it all, Enid being terribly proud of her brave sister and Lionel thankful that he had found a replacement ring for Elsie.

He took the ring out to look at it again. Barbara asked if she might have a look too and he passed it over to her. Unfortunately, it didn't quite make it into her hand and dropped into the glass of coca cola she had in front of her.

'Oh, Lionel I am sorry,' she said and fished the ring out of the glass. Using a paper napkin, she rubbed the ring dry.

'My goodness this is shiny,' she remarked and continued to clean the ring.

Jocasta immediately noticed that this was no ordinary ring, it was platinum rather than silver plate.

'Lionel,' she said, 'this is worth a small fortune. How much did you pay for it?'

'One hundred and fifty pounds,' replied Lionel.

'Well, I suspect it's worth ten times that amount at least. You should have it valued.'

Lionel's first thought was to take the ring back to the shop and explain their mistake, but then he thought of the work that needed to be carried out to repair the church clock mechanism or even the roof. Surely that would do more good and besides, he still had to get a ring to Elsie. He didn't know what to do.

Barbara, who was normally imperturbable, became very excited. Her voice trembling, she exclaimed that he must get it valued and she had thought of a plan.

This would involve driving into London where she knew of a good jeweller near Hatton Garden. She trusted him to give them an honest appraisal of its worth and who knows, he may even buy it. At least with a valuation, Lionel would be in a good position to make his mind up about what to do.

Lionel considered her plan and admitted that, yes, it made good sense, but, when could they go? Barbara suggested they act promptly before Elsie came back. It was soon agreed they would travel to London a couple of days after getting back to Welling-by-the-Sea.

The two days in between arriving home and setting off again would give Barbara enough time to check the various things in her vehicle that need to be checked before embarking on a long journey. She had every confidence in Ruby.

The journey back to Welling-by-the-Sea proved largely uneventful. Sid agreed to drop everyone off at their houses, or as close to them as he could get. It was getting late, but surely these people would find it in their hearts to give him some generous tips? He had, after all, endured more abuse in two days than most coach drivers experience in a lifetime.

To relieve themselves of boredom from the long journey, Jonathon and Jayne suggested they set up a WhatsApp group. This would enable them all to keep in contact and perhaps plan another trip. It turned out that nearly everyone apart from Sid and Josie had a smartphone and so, together, they set up a group called "Antique Wellies" and made sure everyone had access.

Norman wasn't quite sure what WhatsApp was and how he should use it. Jayne assured him it was just like text messaging, but with lots of other people in a conversation, and they could send pictures if they so desired.

Marcus and Jocasta were the first to be dropped off outside their large, fully lit, mock Georgian, executive house. The double electric gates swung open as Marcus pressed the button on the remote control and Sid drove up to the front door.

'Well thank you all very much,' Jocasta said addressing everyone, then rather falsely, went on to say, 'we've had a wonderful time and look forward to the next shopping trip' and, with that, they disembarked and made their way to their front door.

Sid noted "no tip" as he edged his way past the Mercedes and Mini.

Reginald and Diane were next to be dropped off further down the road as the housing changed from larger houses to smaller semi-detached properties closer to town and the schools. They too hadn't bought anything so were able to jump off the coach after saying their goodbyes to everyone.

Eventually, all the passengers were dropped off and Sid could finally drive home with his thirty-pound tip from Agatha, Enid, Lionel, and Barbara. Norman's tip had been to tell him to not drive so fast in future and get his eyes tested.

7. The Trip to London

Barbara had checked Ruby's tyre pressures, water level, oil and screen wash. Her confidence was high that these were all at the required levels. She started Ruby, but just as she did so Annette Digby shot out of her house and across the road banging on the passenger window.

'Are you going away? I mean, it's not Monday when you normally go shopping. It's Thursday and I wondered if everything was ok, or, if you needed something – has something happened?' she enquired.

'Mrs Digby.' The use of formal language intentionally signalling Barbara's displeasure and annoyance at not being able to leave her house without being questioned did not go unnoticed and Annette Digby stepped back

'I am giving Lionel a lift in order that we may conduct some church business today.'

Just as she finished speaking Lionel arrived, checking his pocket watch for the time. Mrs Digby stepped aside as Lionel got into the back of the car. This in itself looked strange to Mrs Digby, but before she had a chance to say anything Lionel, wound the window down and muttered:

'God Speed Mrs Digby – Barbara, foot to the metal.'

Fearful of any further delays, Barbara obliged. She selected reverse and backed out of the drive, then straight into forward and foot hard down on the accelerator. Ruby lurched and those around could hear the sound of her CVT transmission working up to speed. Barbara was thankful that Ruby's clutch did not choose today to slip.

Three minutes later they arrived at Norman's house. He was ready and jumped into the front of the car.

'Now Lionel, I hope you remembered the ring?' he jokingly asked. It was a good question and Lionel was relieved to find he had the ring on him.

Within an hour they were on the M1 and headed into London. They passed Marcus and Jocasta's Brent Cross shopping centre and then drove from there into town before parking in a multi-storey car park.

Barbara was sure Ruby was too old to be bothered or affected by ULEZ. She was, after all, road tax exempt and thanks to her excellent, long-lasting, Dutch-build quality, earned herself the luxury of being eligible for classic car insurance. This helped keep her running costs low and endeared her to Barbara. Ruby had survived two scrappage schemes and was now assured of her place in the history of unremarkable classic car motoring.

Barbara parked the car and they made their way to the jewellers.

Peering in through the door, Barbara pressed the buzzer. A click was heard and the door lock was released.

Inside, the shop was dark, despite three huge chandeliers hanging down from the ceiling. The walls were dark green. The chandeliers were on a dimmer which was only increased to full power when there was the possibility of something of value being bought. For sales they were turned down.

Large mahogany display cabinets were arranged across the back of the shop and to the sides. Behind them was a thoroughfare for shop assistants to glide up and down serving customers. On top of the cabinets were dark red leather mats for customers to inspect items and the walls were adorned with clocks of all sizes and descriptions, the ticking adding to the faded grandeur of what must have been at one time, a very grand shop.

The only customer today was a rather tall lady wearing oversize ruby earrings. Anyone looking closely would have noticed they were in fact cufflinks that she had adapted to her own needs! She was not dissimilar to *The Green Lady* in Tretchikoff's famous painting, except she had quite a lot of make-up on. The lady looked up and smiled pleasantly at all three of them before continuing to inspect a display of rings and tiaras. She often came into this shop as she enjoyed arguing with the owner, Danny Kray, and bought a lot of his cheaper jewellery for her drag act. She had originally thought his surname was Kaye and was most disappointed when she learnt his real name.

Barbara asked if Mr Hoffman was available. It transpired that he had retired and sold the business to Danny Kray, to whom she was now speaking.

Danny had decided to keep the name Joseph Hoffman and Sons over the door as Joe had built up a steady and reputable clientele. Moreover, his own surname brought unfortunate connotations of Reggie and Ronnie Kray. Whilst they weren't relations of his, he did share their passion for getting a deal done.

'Now, how can I help?' asked Mr Kray.

'Well, we wondered if you could take a look at a ring, although I have to say I did think Mr. Hoffman would be here. But if you could take a look and let us know if you think it has any value, well, that really would be most helpful, replied Barbara.

Norman glanced again at the tall lady. He was sure she must be from a local theatre, so tall, so elegant.

Lionel took the ring out of his pocket and placed it on top of the glass cabinet.

Mr Kray increased the lighting in the shop - which caught the attention of the tall lady - and inspected the ring with his monocular.

'Joe's not around today. I'm sorry lady, but I don't think this is worth very much at all. It's shiny for sure but more likely to be costume jewellery. I'd happily take it off your hands for a hundred quid though.' And with that the lighting was reduced to 50%.

'Scooze me,' piped up the Tall Lady, 'but don't be fooled by him, he a crook. It's probably worth far more. Give here, let me look.'

Intrigued, Norman ventured, 'and you are?'

'My name is Paaais Milaaan, I know all about costume jewellery, I get bought enough!' and with that, she let out a huge shrieking laugh.

Paaais Milaaan was in fact Meneer Willem Van Der Veen. As Van Der Veen literally means 'from the swamp', he had decided to adopt his professional name 'Paris Milan' in everyday life. Paris after the home of his favourite hotel and Milan after a rather memorable fashion show in which he almost made it onto the catwalk.

Paris' father was a pianist. Born in the Netherlands, he'd met his wife in Cuba. She was an unaccomplished performer, who believed she could sing. Unfortunately, this was not the case and she was often mistaken for Margarita Pracatan.

The young Willem adored his parents. All three of them travelled throughout Europe, his parents securing gigs wherever they could.

Willem's first drag character in the Netherlands, he named Lieke Vinke (Little Bird). The character immortalised his parents by combining his mother's love of singing with his father's piano playing. Not having received a steady education Willem had failed to be accomplished at either of these skills but possessed an enormous talent to entertain.

So caught up in his character was Willem, that he decided to dress in drag all the time and stay in character, transitioning from Willem to Lieke and then Paris. The other reason was to avoid the debts incurred to American Express as Willem.

Paris' success as a drag queen had, however, not gone unnoticed by several government departments,

particularly since she had forgotten to register for tax or a visa since Brexit. But these were mere details, right now she was interested in the ring and these three charming people.

'Yes, I would say this is Platinum most probably worth a lot of money. Danny you turn the lights up for Paaais please?'

Mr Kray obliged. He wished Paris would just leave his shop. So much time was wasted with this customer and now she had interfered with his chance of making a more than decent profit today.

'Yah, I can see it now, it iz so like ze one I was looking at earlier, only this is real, much better quality – I show you. Danny can you open that cabinet for me please? I show you ze ring.'

Danny did as he was told. There was still a chance that he could make some money today.

Paris showed the other ring to Barbara, Norman and Lionel.

'You see ze difference? Your one is so obviously real and zis other one, well it's good but not ze same class my darlinks.'

'Let me have a closer look at that cheaper one,' said Lionel. He took out his own magnifying glass from his coat pocket and exclaimed:

'Well, I'll be……. It can't be…… It is….. It's a miracle! God in the heavens, how extraordinary. Look Barbara, look at the inscription, it says "Richard and Elsie".'

'Good Lord, so it does, but this couldn't possibly be the ring you married Ben and Lucy with could it?'

'Well, I do believe it is. Elsie was married to Richard and when she called, she said Richard was most annoyed that she had taken her wedding ring off and lost it. This is the ring of that I'm sure. But how did it get here?'

Now, Danny Kray had all his life been the arbitrator of dodgy deals, but he now saw that, in the eyes of god, this was his chance to do good.

'A young couple came in here with that ring. They said it had belonged to an aunt and they needed to sell it to raise some cash as they were going abroad. I felt sorry for them and paid them a hundred pounds for it.'

'I don't believe' countered Paris, 'why you do this for them?'

'Well, believe it or not, that's what happened, Now, tell you what I could do, I'll give you one and a half grand for your ring and you can have that ring in part exchange. How does that sound?'

Before anyone could say anything Lionel agreed and shook hands with Mr Kray. Danny smiled, pleased with the deal and pleased to have helped.

Lionel turned to Paris

'I can't thank you enough Miss Paris. Would you like to join us for lunch?'

'Oh yes please, paaais is hungry and no ring on my finger today, ha ha ha ha!'

The deal concluded and Danny handed over the cash to Lionel in exchange for the platinum ring. All four left the shop happy but hungry.

Barbara remembered she had previously dined in a small Italian pizzeria near the street they were in. All agreed that an Italian late lunch would be most welcome as they could drive back just after the evening rush hour.

It took them ten minutes to arrive at the pizzeria, get seated and order their meals.

'So, Paris, tell me where you are from?' enquired Norman.

Paris recounted the tale of her parents and how she now performed on stage as a drag queen.

'What should we address you as? Are you Mr or Miss?' asked Barbara

'Well, if I am in costume, as I am now and most of ze time, then it is Miss or Paaais, but if I am out of drag then it is Mr or Willem. But that is not very often, if ever.'

'Right,' said Norman. Things were starting to make sense now. He just hoped Paris wouldn't get changed as he loved what she was wearing. She was a stunner no doubt about that. Lionel didn't care. This wonderful lady had found the ring he thought was lost to him forever.

Barbara liked Paris, she had style and an almost vulnerable demeanour once you got past the brash act.

Paris turned to Norman, aware of his admiring glances and asked him what he did for fun.

Norman decided this was his opportunity to impress both Barbara and Paris and found himself saying:

'Oh, I love to sail. I keep a small boat just off the coast. Yes I love it. Hoist the main sail and drop the anchor - or is it the other way round? - anyway, yes sailing absolutely love it. Wind in your hair, the smell of diesel and salt in the sea. Glorious!'

'Norman, you didn't tell me you could sail? How wonderful. You must take me out sometime,' said Barbara.

'Oh absolutely, I would love to,' he replied.

'Oh my god, where iz your boat Norman? You do me big favour and take me somewhere?' asked Paris.

'Well yes, of course. Where is it you want to go?'

'The Netherlands, iz not far but I need go.'

Norman was rather uncomfortable now. He had gotten carried away with his sailing story, never for once imagining that someone might actually want to go with him. He tried to backtrack and say that actually he was carrying out maintenance at the moment, but Paris seemed so keen and he hated the thought of letting her down, let alone Barbara.

Not for the first time, he thought there can't be much to this sailing lark. His brother had been a total idiot all his life and had managed it, just how difficult could it be? He had, after all, been on the boat and seen him start the engine, had seen the sails go up – he remembered pulling a rope somewhere... No it could not be any more difficult than driving a car.

Paris decided she ought to explain why she needed to sail to the Netherlands rather than go by more conventional forms of travel. She recounted how she had been booked to perform her act on a visiting cruise ship. The ship had pulled into Antwerp, and she had given the performance of her life. This was not as Paris Milan, but as Lieke Vinke (little bird). Lieke was a character she sometimes used if she was in a Glam Rock sort of mood. Lieke was a cross between Mark Bolan and Shirley Bassey. Due to the name, Lieke was reserved for the Netherlands only.

After the performance she had been invited for drinks by one of the passengers, a Mr Cruickshaw from Chipping Melchett in the Cotswolds. He was a retired tax inspector or so he'd told her. She found him both attractive and funny so had no hesitation in accompanying him to the bar where the two of them got extremely drunk. Later he invited her to his cabin.

Paris had explained to Mr Cruickshaw that she was a good girl and never visited passengers in their cabins and in any case it was against the rules. However on this occasion, if he didn't say anything, she wouldn't. Unfortunately for them both the intoxicating liquor had gone straight to both their heads and despite Paris's better judgement she went to his cabin whereupon they opened more champagne and drank merrily until the early hours.

At some point, Paris thought she must have revealed to Mr. Cruickshaw that "she" was in fact "he" and that this was an act. She remembered he was chasing her around the cabin.

Anyway, the last thing she remembered was falling over, so she must have knocked herself out.

When she came to in the morning, Mr Cruickshaw was dead! Paris didn't know at the time that he had been diagnosed as having only a few weeks left to live. He had been determined to spend what little time he had left partying his way into the afterlife. The effect of too much alcohol and chasing this lovely lady around his cabin had just been too much and the perfect way for him to depart this mortal coil.

Through the haze of her hangover, the next sound Paris remembered hearing was the foghorn announcing their departure from Antwerp.

What should she do? She had no papers on her, only her bag with some money and her credit card. Her passport was at her parents' house hidden under the floorboards along with her secret stash of space cookies.

She'd decided that the best thing to do was to find somewhere to hide.

Cold and desperate, Paris found her way to the crew cabins on the lower decks and sneaked into an empty one.

Her plan, she explained, had been to keep herself hidden until they arrived in Dover, which she'd understood was the next stop. Dover to Antwerp is roughly a day so it wouldn't be too long to keep herself out of trouble.

After a couple of hours in the cabin it struck her that as the authorities would be after Lieke Vinke dressed in a rather glamorous formal evening dress, she should try and disguise herself. But how?

She'd found a male uniform in the locker of the cabin and got changed into it. Sadly she'd had to take her make-up and wig off but she did at least look part of the crew. Perhaps this would do? But thinking it through she would have to disembark through the crew exit routes. No, she needed to assume an identity.

It was now breakfast time and many of the passengers would be in the dining room with the stewards going in and out of cabins. She left the crew quarters and went to the passenger decks. One of the cabin doors had been left open and she could see a Louis Vuitton suitcase in the hallway ready to be collected. Quickly she entered the cabin and closed the door – the bed hadn't been made so she needed to act quickly.

Inside the case was a coat and a beautiful La Foi burgundy velvet jump suit. This was perfect for her disguise. Looking through the bedside drawers she found four pairs of sunglasses so she helped herself to a pair of Ray Bans. In the bathroom, amongst the many bottles and potions, she found some black hair dye and some makeup that she was sure wouldn't be missed. Perfect. She would look like Jackie Onassis by the time she was ready to leave the ship.

She went onto explain that back in Mr Cruickshaws cabin the transformation from Lieke back into Paris took place in just a few hours. She'd stuck a "do not disturb" notice on the door and pulled a sheet over poor Mr Cruickshaw. By the time she had cleared up she was ready to face the world. By then it was late afternoon and getting dark. She would spend the rest of the trip on the deck, wrapped up in the coat and with the scarf she had in her bag, covering her head.

Eventually, the ship pulled into Dover under cover of darkness. Paris could see passengers making their way to the exit stairs, so she went down and tried to mingle with them.

Fortunately, they had chosen not to check her documents leaving the ship - this would be later - and she was wished a pleasant onward journey.

Once in the main terminus building, things became more awkward. Passports were being checked, papers were being handed over, luggage could be seen arriving, it was very busy.

Walking in front of her, with a trolley full of suitcases, was a porter. His trolley appeared heavy, and he was struggling to keep it from rolling forward as he went down the slight incline towards the barriers.

Ropes had been placed on either side of the pathway to Passport Control. Unlike airports, this was a much simpler process, the ships know who is on board and who is going ashore. In order to avoid Passport Control and break free Paris needed to get under the ropes. What she needed was a diversion and she soon came up with one. She'd noticed the poor porter had loose fitting trousers. As she tapped him on the shoulder she looked up to the heavens and muttered 'god forgive me'. The porter looked round, but Paris had her hands on the top of his trousers and yanked them down.

The porter was shocked, his trousers were down exposing his Santa Claus boxer shorts, he had never been so embarrassed. Unfortunately, he had let go of the trolley and this went hurtling towards passport control. People dodged out of the way quickly. Not so lucky were the party of four people in wheelchairs who were approaching the checkpoint. The trolley - slowing down by this point - pushed all four of them through passport control and into the main concourse.

People were everywhere! Luckily no one was hurt. The trolley had fallen over, suitcases had burst buckles and emptied their loads on the floor. The sight of the expensive contents brought out the worst in people's greed, many of them rushed over to grab whatever they could. Fortunately, the wheelchair occupants weren't hurt but missed out on acquiring any of the suitcase loot.

The bursting suitcases and uncontrolled wheelchairs provided just the diversion Paris needed. She hopped under the rope and disappeared through the main concourse and out into the Dover night air.

Relieved that she was now off the boat, Paris got a taxi to the train station so that she could catch a train to London. She would stay in London whilst she came up with a plan to get back. She had friends in Soho who would help her. The rest, as they say, is history. Paris got to London, and her friends offered her some work doing her new act in the various pubs and clubs around Soho.

'So, you see it been very traumatic for me,' Paris concluded.

'Yes but what happened to the man who died?' asked Barbara.

'Oh, zat norty man! I saw in ze paper he die of heart attack and was expecting it, he very ill – he should have told me before getting me drunk.'

'So you're not wanted by the police and have done nothing wrong?' asked Lionel

'No, but vizout my passport I can't get back home to ze Netherlands. My only way back is by private boat, and I need to get to my parents' house in Amsterdam to get passport to get back into this country legally.'

'Why can't they just send it to you?' asked Barbara.

'Is not that easy, it ees 'idden underneath zeir floor in a air tight tin viz my private stash of space cookies. Zey would disown me if they found them.'

Barbara looked puzzled about the cookies, but Norman decided, cometh the hour, cometh the man.

'In that case, we have to rise to the challenge,' he exclaimed.

Paris looked up and briefly smiled. The other three were exhausted, it was a terrible tale. Poor Paris, they really must try and help her.

It was agreed that Paris should come back to Welling-by-the-Sea with them where they would make arrangements to sail to Antwerp in Norman's boat. From Antwerp, Paris could easily get back to Amsterdam and recover her passport before hopefully joining them for the journey back.

Before she could go with them, however, she needed to make a quick phone call to the pub and her friends with whom she was staying. She would explain that she needed to go away unexpectedly for a few days but would be back soon. Paris popped out of the restaurant to make the call and came back in smiling. All was well with the world, and these were lovely new friends.

Very soon they were making their way back to Ruby and the multi-storey car park.

Barbara started to apologise to Paris about her small car and that it was rather old. Paris yelped with delight when she saw it, her parents had had one and they were built in the Netherlands. It was a sign they were all meant to meet and embark on this great adventure.

Once everyone was in Ruby, Barbara drove them out of the car park, through London, past Brent Cross and out onto the M1.

8. What else can go wrong?

Everyone in the car was quiet. They'd had a long day. Lionel was pleased with the ring swap and that he'd secured enough funds to fix the church clock, possibly even have some left over for the roof.

Barbara felt pleased she'd helped both Lionel and now Paris and was very much looking forward to the trip to Antwerp. It wasn't quite the cruise she had wanted but Norman was entertaining, and she was sure his boat would be quite luxurious, or at least she hoped it would be. How lovely it was to have a man in her life who was a doer, someone she could look up to.

Paris was pleased that, finally, she wouldn't have to worry about her passport and being in the country illegally.

Norman was not so happy; he still had the small matter of learning to sail. It was suddenly all becoming real, he had no time to practice or get lessons.

Ruby was starting to feel the pressure of not the usual one adult - and more recently two - in the car but now four and being on the motorway in the dark.

She wasn't used to this; she was a classic and a retired one at that. She was meant to potter up the road to the shopping centre and the church.

Finally, it was all too much and one of Ruby's rubber belts that provided power to the back wheels snapped. Tic tic tic weeeeeeee came the noise then another tic tic tic weeeee as the other belt snapped under the pressure of being the sole driving belt.

Barbara steered Ruby into the hard shoulder and she came to a standstill.

'What's wrong with it?' asked Norman

'I don't know,' replied Barbara, 'but we need to call for help.'

Barbara fished out her mobile phone and called her breakdown company.

'Where are you exactly madam and what appears to be the problem? Would you say you are vulnerable?' came the reply from the disinterested operator.

'I am on the M1 on the hard shoulder near junction 5, I think. My car made funny noises. I think it's something serious as I lost power, but the engine is still running. Maybe the gearbox? There are four of us in the car,' she winked at Norman before continuing,

'I have a cranky old man next to me, a man of the cloth in the back and a drag queen in the car. My vehicle is forty years old and I am extremely tired. I would say we are vulnerable.'

'Right thank you, madam, I have that. One of our patrol vehicles will be with you shortly. If you need an update you can go to our website and enter your registration number. Would you like to take part in our customer service quality assurance survey? If so please press one when I have finished this call. Thank you.' And with that, the agent hung up.

'Well, I suppose we wait now,' said Barbara.

And wait they did. Half an hour, then an hour. Eventually a large van with flashing amber lights pulled up behind them.

After a ten-minute inspection of the car the breakdown engineer gleefully advised Barbara that the car could not be fixed at the roadside and needed to go to a specialist.

'Well in that case, can you tow us back to the garage at Welling-by-the-Sea?' asked Barbara.

'I'm sorry madam but the terms of your breakdown cover are for a tow of up to ten miles to a garage we approve of. We are so busy tonight that we can't allow you to upgrade your membership.'

This was ridiculous! Barbara remembered reading somewhere about the ten-mile limit but hadn't thought it that important.

It was agreed that the car would be towed to a nearby town and the breakdown company arranged with the garage for the car to be looked at in the morning. In the meantime, the patrol man could drop them off at a nearby hotel he knew of and they could continue their journey once the car had been fixed.

By the time the car had been dropped the group of four were extremely tired. The hotel turned out to be a B&B run by the patrol man's sister, Patricia.

As they climbed the steps leading to the front door, Lionel glanced to his right and admired the front window with its large picture of a single horse racing around a track. The painting was on an easel, lit up from below.

Barbara rang the bell and shortly afterwards the door opened. The breakdown driver shouted out to the lady in the open doorway:

'Pat love, done you a favour. I got these customers for you. They just need to stay over tonight, I know you said things are slow right now – see ya!' And with that, he drove off.

Pat looked down at them. She wondered if Lionel was in a fancy dress. Paris she could tell was in drag, but the old man and woman, hmm, she had a feeling this was going to be awkward.

'I say, there's quite a crowd of us tonight! lovely' said a formal-looking man suddenly coming up the stairs behind them.

'Thomas, leave my guests alone. Come on in, you're in room nine tonight.'

Pat looked again at the group. Oh dear she was going to have to explain that her boarding house was in fact a house of unconventional entertainment and therapy. She'd told her family it was a B&B, but these poor people looked so completely worn out she didn't have the heart to turn them away.

'Look, I'm sorry but this is a bit of an unconventional B&B. The girls and I offer bespoke entertainment and therapy services to a rather exclusive clientele who pre-book. However, as I am working tonight you are welcome to stay in my flat at the top of the stairs. There are three spare bedrooms and a sofa, I'll show you up.'

'That really is very kind of you,' said Barbara. She was totally worn out now. Lionel blessed her and Paris pursed her lips and gave Pat a disapproving look. Paris didn't approve of her newfound innocent friends staying in this sort of "establishment".

Paris needn't have worried as the flat at the top of the stairs was very well appointed. Pat showed them around before leaving them to sort themselves out.

Fortunately, the three spare bedrooms had been freshly made up by Pat's cleaner earlier that week. Lionel, Barbara and Paris took one each, leaving Norman with the sofa. He didn't mind as he said it would be better since he could protect the ladies better from this vantage point. He doubted he would sleep much anyway. Pat had given them fresh towels and toothbrushes, so they had everything they needed for a comfortable night's sleep.

Norman asked if anyone would care for a nightcap. He had had the foresight to bring a small bottle of whisky with him for emergencies. Everyone agreed that a nightcap would be most welcome.

'Well we've had quite a day,' remarked Barbara.

"I am sooo pleased I met with you all and you are to become my friends. I cannot believe my good luck,' answered Paris. Her wig was starting to itch and she thought that as it had been a long day, now would be a good time for bed so they could all wake up fresh in the morning.

One by one they used the bathroom and went to bed. Barbara stopped to give Norman a kiss on the cheek and wish him good night. For the first time in many years Norman felt warm inside and a sense of belonging. It didn't matter that he was sleeping on a sofa in a strange house, with a vicar in one room and a drag queen in another - he was starting to feel alive and wanted.

Paris did not sleep easily in strange places and tonight was no exception. At around two in the morning she could hear what sounded like someone being slapped in the room below her and the words:

'On my arris, my arris, nanny!'

And then, 'I'm trying, I'm trying, take that you naughty boy!'

'I say, oh nanny, I am so sorry for not eating my dinner.'

'Yes you have been a naughty boy haven't you? Well, we shall have to punish you some more.'

'On my arris, oh please on my arris!'

Half asleep Paris thought the man was calling out for her. She got out of bed and crept out of her room and through the sitting room past a snoring Norman.

Paris remembered to snip the latch so she could get back in. On the landing she could hear the pained cultured voice again screaming:

'Nanny my arrris, oh my poor arris!'

'You've been such a naughty boy, it's time for the cane I'm afraid. Now where did I put it? Let me see, could it be in my top drawer? Yes I think it is.'

And with that Paris threw the door open ready to hear why someone was calling her name with such vigour.

The sight that greeted her was not for the feint hearted. The first thing she saw was the man she had met on the stairs earlier. A certain Thomas Whitmore. Thomas was in his sixties, he had a good shock of very light grey hair and a tan. He ran the local, family-owned since 1824, department store in town called Whitmore and Sons. Thomas was the son and the last member of the family to run it. He had never married but had had a string of girlfriends. His belief that all relationships can only have seven meaningful years had backfired on him. Thomas had met Pat when she came to place a substantial order of furniture from him and they had become friends.

The image Paris had of Thomas was of a sixty-something still in the suit he had worn on the stairs. She could see his moustache curling above his upper lip. As he had no glasses on he was straining to see Paris's face.

The other occupant of the room was Miss June Blomfield, a pretty thirty-something lady wearing a white apron over a duck egg blue dress, comfortable shoes and with her blonde hair restrained under a small brown cap.

'Who are you?' she asked.

'I am Paris Milan. I heard my name being called.'

'I say,' piped up Thomas. 'Two Nannies.'

At that moment Pat came out of the room she was in.

'What's going on?' she asked. 'Mr Whitmore, I do apologise for the – ahem – interruption.'

'Paaais heard her name and came to see who call her.'

June decided enough was enough and told Paris to leave or she would have to beat her out of the room, emphasising her point by pulling her cane out of the drawer. On seeing the instrument of punishment, Paris put her hand out and grabbed the end of it from June. June let go all to easily and Paris stumbled backwards hitting her head on the wall before falling to the ground.

'Oh Nanny, I feel I've been a very naughty boy,' Thomas mumbled a bit too excitedly.

'Right enough's enough,' said Pat, deciding that she needed to take control of the situation.

'You lady, get up and come with me. And you two, close the door and get back to doing whatever it was you were doing.'

Pat took Paris's hand and got her to her feet before they left the room and closed the door on Thomas and June.

'Thomas has been such a naughty boy where shall I punish him?' June asked.

'Oh Nanny, on my arris, on my arris,' came the reply.

Paris looked at Pat, opened her mouth to say something, but thought better of it and was marched upstairs before being dropped off at the flat door.

'Now, I don't want to hear another word out of you lot, you could have cost me one of my best customers. Never complains unless he's meant to, does Mr Whitmore. And he always tips handsomely, lovely man.'

Paris shook her head to show she understood and went to her room. She could still hear slapping and her name being called. Why he would still want to call her, she had no idea. Eventually she fell asleep.

As the sun started to rise, all four occupants of the top floor flat were awoken by a knock on the door and the words:

'Open up, this is the police.'

As Norman had been sleeping on the sofa he was the closest to door and opened it to let the police officer in.

'What's all this about?' he asked

The policeman explained they were carrying out a raid on the establishment as it was suspected of being a house of ill repute.

Barbara came out of her room and caught the end of the conversation.

'What's going on? What is this?' she asked.

'Are you in charge here?' asked the policeman.

'No, I am not,' Barbara replied, 'we are simply staying overnight as my car broke down and the patrol man dropped us off here.'

Paris and Lionel both choose the same moment to exit their rooms and the policemen raised an eyebrow.

'What now?' exclaimed Paris. 'All night I hear slap, slap, slap and screams from downstairs and now we have man in fancy dress as Policeman. It all too much for Paaais.'

Lionel stretched his arms in the air, it had been a long night. As he did so, the wad of money he had received for the ring fell to the floor.

'Right, that's it, you're all under arrest on suspicion of running a disorderly house. Sergeant Doherty, read them their rights.'

Sergeant Doherty did indeed read them their rights although Paris didn't really understand. Barbara thought it best to keep quiet, Lionel was glad he had retired and Norman was worried about his past record.

Sergeant Doherty then escorted them down the stairs and they were bundled into a waiting police van alongside the other occupants of the disorderly house.

Things were not entirely calm inside the van. Pat was demanding the Police let them go as she knew some very influential people. Thomas had decided it would be in his best interests to inform the police of his good standing in the community. How he wished he'd listened to Nanny and met a nice girl at one of the many country house parties he had been invited to as a young man.

'I don't belong in here,' he said. 'I am Thomas Whitmore of Whitmore and Sons. If you call my home ask for a lady called – ahem – Nanny. She will tell you I have never been here before and that I must have sleepwalked or someone drugged me.'

He wasn't too worried as he knew everyone thought him odd. It wasn't helped he supposed by retaining the services of his now very elderly nanny, yes that might seem strange to some people. Nonetheless, he wouldn't want to fall out of favour with Nanny. How he wished he was safe in the top floor nursery of his house sipping tea with her.

Paris was extremely quiet. She thought this was it, this was the end. She was so close to leaving the country and getting her passport and now, this. The shame of it all. To make matters worse her wig was itching like crazy and she really needed a good scratch. She gingerly put a finger underneath it to have a scratch which made it look as if the top of head was loose.

Lionel was wondering what on earth he had done to deserve this and why he was being arrested. He wished his faith endorsed rosary beads as right now he would find it a comfort. As he didn't have any he fiddled with the chain on his pocket watch

Norman held Barbara's hand. He thought showing his caring side to Barbara and the police would show him in a better, more caring light to both authorities.

Arriving at the Police Station they were all taken to a large cell for processing. The officer in charge decided to start with the suspect least likely to be involved in a solicitous act so he called on Barbara.

He was really looking forward to interviewing some of the others, at least one of them was a celebrity and he could get a promotion out of the arrests.

Barbara explained exactly what had happened and ran through the fact that they were on their way back to Welling-by-the-Sea when their car had broken down. The officer quizzed her on the money that they had found hidden in Lionel's robes. She explained that they had sold a ring in London to a jeweller called Mr Kray, then on the way back her car had broken down. It couldn't be fixed until the morning and the patrol man had dropped them off at the B&B. The officer could ring Mr Kray if he wanted.

'Mr Kray! You have got to be kidding me, I suppose you are going to tell me that the vicar is really a vicar, and the other lady is a drag queen?'

'Actually, Kray really is his name and you can call him. You can also call the Bishop of Chillington to check that Lionel is a vicar, or rather he is a retired vicar. The WI will vouch for me and I will vouch for Norman and Paris. While you're at it, call my breakdown company and check that we really did breakdown and here's the number of the garage – ask about Ruby if you would be so kind.'

The officer had heard it all, what a rude woman! Keen to resolve the matter, he nonetheless did as he was told. This woman reminded him of a schoolmistress he was rather scared of when he was a child. She had the same eyes and sharp little nose.

Enquiries complete and satisfied that the four really didn't have anything to do with the house of ill repute, the officer decided to release them with a caution. He couldn't wait to start on the real culprits. Oh how he was looking forward to this. It would be something to tell the lads at Sunday's rugby game. Sadly, it was not to be, Pat, had been telling the truth, she really did offer a service catering for people requiring bespoke entertainment services. One of her guests for example loved playing the Muppets, he would dress up as a Kermit with Pat in a Miss Piggy outfit. No charges were forthcoming.

Paris was extremely relieved as she lit a cigarette on the steps of the Police station. That was until she was tapped on the shoulder.

'Paris? Paris Milan?' she heard.

As she spun round she saw another tall officer with a beaming face.

'Joey!' she blurted out. 'What are you doing here?'

Joey was a regular visitor to one of her west end gigs. He and his friends were always such lovely guests, and she took great delight in embarrassing them by asking them to get on the stage or sitting on their laps whilst she sang to the audience.

'What do you think I'm doing here? I'm a policeman. Now then Paris, I heard about what happened to you. Honestly, what are you like? Anyways, I'm glad you're all right. I understand you and your friends need to get to the garage up the road – now, it's not regular but it would be my pleasure to give you all a lift in my panda car, not to mention my turn to embarrass you!'

Paris gratefully accepted and they were dropped off at the garage.

The proprietor of the garage, Jack Bottomley, had assumed that today would be like any other day. He'd received the email from the breakdown company last night about Ruby and had contacted one of his friends who ran a Volvo spares company. Luckily, he had a couple of drive belts for the car and had them couriered over so they would be waiting for him at the Garage. One hour later and feeling very pleased with himself he had Ruby fixed and ready to go. All he needed now was for the owner to arrive.

And arrive she did. The sight of the police car, with its lights flashing, pulling up onto the kerb made him wonder about some of the less-than-above-board deals he had been involved in a few years ago.

Out of the front of the police car emerged a very be-draggled Paris.

"What the….?" thought Jack. And then out of the back emerged a vicar. That was it, no more home brew for Jack.

Finally squeezing out of the back came Barbara and Norman.

Barbara again took charge and introduced herself whilst she patted an almost beaming Ruby on the bonnet.

Barbara went into the office and settled her bill, thanking Jack for the extraordinarily good service. Lionel blessed Jack – he wasn't sure why he kept feeling the need to bless people, but it had been an unusual few days.

Settled back into Ruby, Barbara started the engine and they were on their way. Surely now they could get home.

9. Home at last

It was almost three o'clock by the time the four of them arrived at Welling-by-the-Sea.

As they pulled into Barbara's road, Mrs Digby, who had been at her kitchen window, ran out to greet them. She wanted to know what church business they had been on and why two people had left and four returned.

Mrs Digby knocked on the car window.

'Oh, I see you're back. Did you have a good time? Where did you go? Where did you stay last night? Oh my, Barbara, you don't look well. Lionel you don't look well either. Norman why did you get into her car? I thought you said you would never go near that car again. And who's this??'

'Mrs Digby, I'm sure you mean well but this really isn't the time. We are all extremely tired and it's been a long day. Now if you don't mind,' said Barbara.

Unfortunately, Mrs Digby did mind, she had to find out what had been going on. Paris sensed that this lady was causing a problem. She opened her door and stepped out. What greeted Mrs Digby was very far removed from the last word in sophistication. Paris's hair by now looked like a swarm of bees had taken nest in it. The gel she had applied yesterday morning to keep her wig in place had melted. In the course of doing so, it had slowly dripped down her face making her makeup run. Her eyeliner was smudged making it look as if she had two black eyes, and the front of her dress was crumpled and stained from the coffee she had spilt on herself whilst in the police station.

Suddenly, Paris felt an itch in her hair. It was her Amy Winehouse wig - or as she liked to call it, her Amy Housewine look. Paris batted the wig with one hand whilst a bemused Mrs Digby looked on. Aware of the stare Paris hissed at Mrs Digby. Soon the look of bemusement turned into horror as Paris screamed and tore the wig off her head revealing a bald head. This was too much! Mrs Digby also screamed and ran back into her house. Barbara had brought home a monster!

After some tea and cake, Lionel made his way back to his house across the street. Norman said he was fine to walk home – he could do with the fresh air and besides, he needed to think about how he was going to learn to sail. A good walk would do him the world of good.

Barbara, Norman, and Paris agreed they would leave in a couple of days for the marina where Norman's boat was moored.. Paris would stay with Barbara as this would give them the opportunity to sort out some clothes and makeup for their impending sea voyage.

Norman was in charge of securing provisions; it was his job to make sure they had everything they needed for their upcoming voyage.

97

10. Hoist the Mainsail

The day of their voyage arrived.

Norman, unaware of high tide or low tide times had asked Barbara to pick him up at ten o'clock. This would leave them, plenty of time to load the car and make their way to the marina. It was just lucky for Norman that high tide was at ten o'clock and that the marina didn't suffer too badly from low or high tide.

As Barbara reversed out of her drive and into the road, Lionel rushed over to greet her.

'Morning Barbara. I thought you ought to know, Elsie visited me last night and I was able to give her the ring back, she was most pleased. I really am so grateful to you all for your help – good luck with your trip to Antwerp and we'll see you in a few days.'

'Antwerp?' It was Mrs Digby. She had seen the car reversing and Lionel talking. Having fully recovered from the other day she was keen to learn what today's gossip could be.

Barbara pretended she hadn't heard Mrs Digby and drove off.

It took Barbara, Norman, and Paris an hour to load up the provisions Norman had bought. Once loaded, they were on their way.

It was only a fifteen-minute drive to the marina and Barbara marvelled at the number of ships' masts, it really did give her a true nautical feeling as they drove through the gates. An exciting new adventure was about to start.

'Now the boat is moored on Pontoon C5,' Norman informed them, 'but first, we need to get our supplies to it.'

A trolley was procured, and they loaded up before heading down the pathway to the pontoon.

Norman was starting to get nervous now, but the weight of the trolley and his determination to not let go as they went down the steep pathway meant no one was the wiser.

Norman's brother, Siegfried, had named his boat Westerly Breeze. This rather unimaginative name was due to the boat being a Westerly 35 and it being extremely windy on the day he bought it.

Pontoon C5 was found, and Westerly Breeze located right at the end.

'Oh my goodness she's beautiful' said an admiring Barbara. This was much better than any cruise she could have imagined.

The boat was gleaming. Siegfried had taken great care of her; it was probably the only thing in his life he had taken care of.

Norman stepped aboard and invited Barbara and Paris aboard, holding their hands to ensure they managed to transfer themselves safely from the edge of the pontoon to the deck of the boat.

He wondered what he should do next? Ah, open the cabin up. He fished around in his pocket for the keys and undid the hatch lock. Again, Barbara said how beautiful the boat was and what a lovely interior. Paris too admired the boat and said how wonderful Norman was to help her like this.

As the ladies settled into the cabin and the supplies were brought on board, the tide started to rise and the lines securing Westerly Breeze to the pontoon became taut.

Norman remembered that he needed to disconnect the mains supply which he did and then switched the electrical circuits over to battery. He was remembering everything his brother had done.

Soon the radio was on, the instruments were alive, and he was ready to start the engine. He would motor out on the engine and hopefully that would be enough to get them to Antwerp. No need for sails.

Rather nervously, for his hand was shaking quite a bit, he took the lines off the boat and cast them back onto his finger berth. Westerly Breeze was floating freely and ready to go. The tide gently pushed her into the boat next to him but the fenders made sure there was no damage.

Starter key in his hand he opened the small control panel below one of the seats. He put the key into the ignition switch and immediately a buzzer sounded. That was OK he thought, it was just a warning, I used to hear this all the time.

He pulled the choke out and started the engine. The diesel engine turned over once and spluttered into life. Norman checked that the engine was dispersing cooling water and indeed it was.

'Life jackets on everyone,' he instructed.

They all laughed at how large the life jackets made them look as they tried to work out how to put them on.

Norman proudly put his brother's captain's cap on his head and smiled to himself. He was sure his brother would be proudly watching down on him from heaven.

And that was it. All crew members on deck, safely ensconced in life jackets. All lines released, just the hint of a breeze and the engine was chugging away nicely.

This was going extremely well.

Norman looked at the engine control lever, it was marked Fore and Stern. Remembering that Stern meant reverse he pulled it slowly back into Stern and Westerly Breeze was backing out of her finger berth.

Feeling very pleased with himself Norman patted himself on the back and looked at the smiling faces of Barbara and Paris. He looked up to the skies and uttered,:'Siegfried, there's nothing to this sailing lark.'

He laughed and thought "there really is nothing to this. I mean, all that sailing talk, just how hard can it be?"

Westerley Breeze continued going backwards and Norman turned the wheel - or helm to call it by it's nautical term. Unfortunately as he turned it the boat went in the opposite way to which he wanted. Panicking, he turned the other way and nothing happened.

'Brakes, brakes!' he screamed as he tried to get the engine control lever to neutral. But the boat was now moving and he needed to get the lever into forward. It was too late and they gently hit the boat behind them causing it to crash into the pontoon.

Hearing the crash, people were now starting to gather and watch, as is all too sadly often the way when a novice sailor first attempts manoeuvres at close quarters.

Barbara could see people in the clubhouse looking down and pointing. Paris wished she had dressed more appropriately.

Finally, forward was engaged and the boat slowed before moving forward again. The tide was strong and Norman had not applied enough power, so they soon found themselves drifting back into the space they had just left.

Barbara looked down at the control panel and switched the engine off and they came to a gentle stop in the pontoon bay. A rather kindly berth holder, seeing their difficulties, helped with drawing the boat in and securing her lines.

Barbara looked at Norman and instead of scolding him said, 'You don't know how to sail do you?'

'Well, of course I do, it's just that the tide is so strong and, well, there's something wrong with the controls.'

'Oh just admit it, we are not going anywhere anytime soon. Come on it's getting dark and everyone is watching. Let's go down below and have something to eat and drink.'

Paris looking very disappointed, had to admit that she would rather get to Antwerp in one piece than not at all.

Having decided they couldn't sail the boat themselves that evening and that it was too late to do anything else, they opened a bottle of wine. And then another. And then another.

Barbara, a conservative drinker at the best of times, racked her brains, wondering how they could get out of this mess, and get someone to sail the boat. After her second glass of wine, she remembered a conversation at dinner with Jonathon and Jayne who had said their dream was to buy a boat of their own with the intention of sailing to Europe.

'Eureka!'

She told Paris and Norman about Jonathan and Jayne's plans. Paris suggested maybe they should call them, but sadly neither Barbara or Norman had their telephone numbers.

'Hang on a minute,' slurred Norman, 'couldn't we use that What's thingy they installed on our phones?'

'Now you are starting to make sense,' replied Barbara and with that she sent her first group WhatsApp message asking for Jonathan and Jayne to get in contact with her if they fancied an adventure, sailing a boat to Antwerp. She stressed they would be relying on their sailing skills as neither Barbara, Norman nor Paris had any idea how to sail a boat, let alone navigate to the Netherlands.

Luckily, a surprised but delighted, Jonathan and Jayne did fancy an adventure and were free to join them the next day. They had heard about the ring and Paris from their neighbour who had been caught by Annette Digby on the way to the newsagents.

After a restless night's sleep Barbara, Norman and Paris awoke to an insistent tapping on the side of the boat.

'Ahoy there captain, permission to come aboard?' shouted Jonathon.

'Yah, 'urry up,' replied Paris. 'Captain 'e still asleep but Paaais says come aboard.'

Barbara was awake and dressed and trying to get the stove to light. She climbed the stairs, pleased to see Jonathan and Jayne, and goodness me did they look the sailing part. Was that Versace they were wearing? Their blue and white horizontal striped tops matched their white trousers and deck shoes perfectly. Paris was also impressed, wishing again she had something better to wear.

Norman was now awake and relieved to see Jonathan and Jayne.

'Dear boy, I handover Captains' responsibility to you,' he said, beaming.

'Actually, it's me who will be your Captain,' said Jayne, smiling as she looked at Norman. 'I captained an all-female crew around the south of France a few years ago and can't wait to get started. I shall be helping Jonathan perfect his skills. '

There were now five souls aboard Westerley Breeze and cabins were allocated. Unfortunately, there were only three cabins. Jonathan and Jayne had the double, Paris one of the singles and Barbara the other. Norman was left with the table seat which doubled as a berth in the main cabin. It was opposite the galley so at least he could make himself some tea if he got up in the night.

Jayne immediately set about getting everyone organised and briefing them on their individual tasks. She plotted a route, ensured that the radio and safety systems on board were working, and insisted everyone wore their life jackets and that they knew what to do in the unlikely event of an emergency.

By eleven o'clock they were ready to go.

'OK Jonathan, do you want to take us out?' Jayne asked her husband.

'Oh rather, super, great, yah.'

'Well assume the position then.'

And with that Jonathan knelt down behind the helm, so that he was facing the back of the boat with Jayne crouching behind him, her fingers touching his temples. Aware that the others were looking at them rather strangely she told them that this was how they did things. Jonathan liked to be relaxed when he was at the helm as it helped him concentrate.

'Goodness' remarked Barbara, not all together sure this was the way Cunard sailed their ships.

Paris was ready with the controls and she started the engine on Jayne's command.

Jayne started rubbing Jonathan temples and chanting 'nom nom nom','nom nom nom'.

Jonathan took a deep breath, looked at Paris and said 'Stern Slowly.'

A rather puzzled Paris replied:

'What you mean STERN? Paris smiling, happy we go, yes?'

'I mean put the boat into reverse. Backwards, we need to go backwards.'

'Oh why you no say backwards then? get Paaais confused!'

Jayne could sense Jonathan was starting to get stressed, his shoulders were tensing up. She hoped it wasn't too late. 'nom nom nom, my darling, nom nom nom!'

Westerley Breeze eased gently out of her berth turning slowly to the left and on Jonathan's command Paris then put the boat into "Forward". Without hitting anything, the boat continued turning before starting to straighten and move forward. Jonathan jumped up and moved around to the front of the helm so he could see where they were going.

Finally, they were on their way and motoring out into the channel that led to the North Sea.

Barbara couldn't help but let out a cheer and the others soon joined in. Finally, they were on their way,

"Antwerp here we come" shouted Norman looking up at the skies, hoping his late brother, Siegfried, was watching.